Thomas Atwood

The Ship

Thomas Atwood

The Ship

ISBN/EAN: 9783337311971

Printed in Europe, USA, Canada, Australia, Japan

Cover: Foto ©Andreas Hilbeck / pixelio.de

More available books at **www.hansebooks.com**

THE

SHIP "MARY ALICE;"

OR,

MY PRAYERS WILL BE ANSWERED,—GOD WILL SAVE YOU, MY PRECIOUS BOY.

BY

REV. THOMAS ATWOOD.

BOSTON:

FRANKLIN PRESS: RAND, AVERY, & CO.

1878.

PREFACE.

THE Author of this narrative, having spent more than thirty years of his life upon the ocean, and more than twenty years in the Christian ministry, and supposing himself laid upon the shelf for the crime of being an old man, and all income in that direction being cut off, and deprecating idleness even in old age, has written the within narrative, hoping to impress the vast importance of experimental religion upon the minds of every reader, from seeing the rich and ripe clusters of precious fruit which others have gathered for themselves from the vine-tree of Jesus' love. As the gospel-bearing ship "Mary Alice" will begin her history and mission, so the Author sends this narrative abroad, which describes her first voyage around the globe. Her second and subsequent ones may follow the first, if this volume should attract and benefit the reading public.

THE AUTHOR.

CONTENTS.

6 CONTENTS.

THE SHIP "MARY ALICE."

CHAPTER I.

JOHN SHIELDS, the subject of this narrative, was born in Vermont, and lived with his parents, and worked on the farm with his father through all the long summer days. The only education he received was by attending the fall and winter terms of the district school. He had one sister, two years his senior, whom he tenderly loved, and to whom he was very warmly attached: her name was Mary Bliss Shields. When Johnny, as Mary always called him, had any leisure hours, he always sought his sister Mary's company. She was his only playmate, guide, and counsellor. Their love for each other was of that quality which led them cheerfully to make sacrifices one for the other, if they could administer to each other's happiness by the sacrifices they made; so that, if either of them had presents made them by their friends of nuts and candy, they remained untouched till a division was made between them.

Their parents were not wealthy; yet they owned a snug little farm, which, through their daily industry and economy, had always yielded them something more than a competence for their daily necessities. Mr. Shields and his wife, the parents of Johnny and Mary, were both living, practical Christians. Mr. Shields was an Irish Protestant, and left Ireland in 1825 on account of the terrible persecution to which all Protestants in Ireland were at that time subjected, and was at the time he landed in B——, only twenty years of age. Remaining in B—— a few days, he thought it would be better to go into the

country, and try to learn some good trade which he believed would secure to him a good living. He started out
on foot, depending upon God's providence to guide him,
and open the way. He came into the town of W——,
where he hired himself to a Mr. H——, to blow and strike
in his blacksmith-shop. Mr. H—— soon found him to be
a good, steady, industrious man, and he made a contract
with him; and Mr. Shields continued to work for Mr.
H——, receiving his board and twenty dollars per month
for his services.

At the close of the two years Mr. Shields, by his industry and close attention to his business, had become the
best horse-shoer in that vicinity; and Mr. H——, fearing
he might lose him, took him in as partner in his business.
He remained his partner for four years; and in 1831 he
dissolved his partnership with Mr. H——, and went to
Vermont and bought a farm, and erected a blacksmith-
shop in S——, where, during the fall and winter, he
worked at his trade, and attended to his farm in the
summer.

In May, 1832, seven years after he landed in B——,
Mr. Shields married Miss Mary Bliss. She was then
twenty-four, and he was twenty-seven years of age; and I
remark that Mrs. Shields was what every person who
knew her called a consistent Christian. Perhaps none enjoyed the conjugal relation more than did Mr. Shields and
his wife, and he sometimes playfully called her his Blissful Mary. Just eighteen months after their marriage, a
little daughter was given them to gladden their hearts.
The loving father could find no name so sweet to him as
that of his loving wife; and he named her for her mother,
— Mary Bliss Shields. She proved to have inherited her
mother's mild, affectionate, trusting disposition, which
soon made her a little sunbeam of light and love. Two
years after, little Johnny made his appearance in the household to quicken the loving pulses of father, mother, and
sister; and here was found one useful, loving, Christian
family.

Mr. Shields began the world right; and, from the day
of his marriage, he never allowed business, friends, or
any other circumstances within his control, to prevent

him from sustaining his daily family worship; and often told his wife, that at the morning altar he found strength for the duties of the day. Thus his two children were brought up and educated to believe that God's claims upon them were of first importance, and must never be neglected. God and his claims first, and business and the world afterwards, was his motto. The children at an early age attended the sabbath school. Mary, at the age of twelve years, indulged hope in Jesus her Saviour; and, although young, she very soon became a very intelligent and practical Christian. Her mother had discharged her duty faithfully, and now she was reaping the sweet fruitage. Little Mary became very anxious for her dear brother Johnny, that he, too, might know and love the same Saviour who had forgiven her sins, and made her rejoice in Jesus' love. But Johnny, although he had been taught the importance of religion, was so fond of play, that he could not seem to fix his young mind upon the subject.

In January, 1848, Mrs. Shields had taken a severe cold. A fever soon set in, which brought on a terrible cough; and though husband, doctors, children, and neighbors, by whom she was universally beloved, did all that could be done, a quick consumption soon did its work. Her husband's love for her had been so deep, ardent, and tender, that it seemed as though his own life would soon pay the forfeit of his love for her whom he regarded as the best woman upon earth. Mrs. Shields was, in fact, a noble woman, — noble as a wife and mother, noble as a constant, practical, living Christian. The influence of her Christlike spirit was felt not only in her household and the church, but in her neighborhood, and wherever she was known. She had become fully ripe; and her Saviour called her away from the cares and toils of earth to the home of the blessed. After she was taken sick, and felt that she was about to leave those she loved, she felt very anxious for her dear Johnny. She called him to her bedside. He was about fourteen years of age. She said, "My dear boy, your mother will soon leave you, and go to dwell with Jesus. If you were only a Christian, there would not be a pang of sorrow in my leaving

you all. Your dear father and sister, that you love, will
find a home with me in yon bright world of glory whenever Jesus the Master calls them." She then put her
arm around him, and drew him closer to her, and said,
"Remember, and never forget, the words of your dying
mother: Give your heart and your life to Jesus. Trust
in him as your sister has, and Jesus will save you as he
did save her. *God will answer my prayers for you. God
will save you, my precious boy.*" The effort she had made
to impress truth upon Johnny's mind weakened her so
much, that she only lingered a few hours; and her last
words were, "All is peace." Peace, indeed, and triumph
and glory, for her, but not so to the bleeding husband and
father's soul. She was buried from the church where she
for years had ever been a consistent member; and, as one
after another looked into that sweet face from which the
victor's smile had not yet departed, each felt that there
was a supporting power in the religion of Jesus to which
this world were strangers.

After the funeral was over, and the grief-stricken ones
had returned to their homes, Mr. Shields called his two
children to him, and said, "Your dear mother has gone
to dwell with the Saviour she so ardently loved, and whom
she so faithfully served. And now, my dear Mary, I wish
to tell you that you have many of your dear mother's
traits of character, I trust, indelibly stamped upon your
heart, as well as her features and form of person; and
my desire is, that you may become as good and useful as
your dear mother was. You will now assume all the
duties of housekeeper, for which your mother has so
faithfully trained and educated you; and I know it will
be your pleasure to try to comfort me in my heart-rending
sorrow. I fear that both of you, my dear loved children,
will soon be left orphans; and I now, therefore, commit
and commend you to my faithful Saviour, who is the
orphans' God. Your dear mother's death will, I fear,
soon be the means of terminating my own existence here
with you. Although in heart I am fully resigned to God's
will in removing my almost idolized wife from earth to
heaven, yet my physical structure has received such a
shock, that I fear it will never rally again to my former

state of health. My farm is unencumbered. I owe no debts. If I should die suddenly, in my desk you will find my bank-book, which claims one thousand dollars in the savings bank in B——. The farm and buildings are worth about four thousand dollars more. Thus you see that you will have something to begin the world with. I have told you how I began life ; and, when I married your mother, I believe I was the happiest man on earth. Should either of you ever marry, I beg of you, under no circumstances, ever to marry any person that is not a living, practical Christian.''

Only one year had passed away after Mr. Shields buried his wife, when he was, by his neighbors, brought home dead. While shoeing a horse, his hammer fell out of his hand, and he fell over backward without uttering a word or groan. The attending physician said he had died with a sudden attack of the heart. Johnny was at work in the yard, sawing wood, when the lifeless body of his father was brought home. So sudden was the announcement, that his sister Mary fainted away. When Johnny saw the body of his dead father, and his apparently lifeless sister, whom he loved even dearer than his own life, he broke down, and cried out in his grief-stricken anguish, '' I am all alone!'' He embraced his sister, saying, '' Mary, my dear sister Mary, do speak to me once more! Speak, dear Mary! Do not leave me alone, my dear sister!'' Oh, how often does the dear Father in heaven send these sharp pangs of sorrow into human hearts, to test, prove, and discipline us, and better fit us to accomplish our mission here upon earth! After an hour's unconsciousness Mary was restored. The neighbors, friends, and their pastor, all gathered around, and deeply sympathized with these lonely orphans, administering consolation and assistance to these children of affliction and sorrow.

These two children had loved their dear mother with all the warm intensity of their young hearts ; but their dear father was left to them, and their hearts clung to him as the running vine clings to the wall. Now he was gone, their last earthly prop had been removed. After the first gush of feeling had subsided, dear trusting

Mary said to her dear brother Johnny, " Jesus is left to us still. Jesus never dies, and will support us, even in this sad affliction. You know, my dear brother, that father and mother both taught us to trust in Jesus ; and his word says, ' They that trust in the Lord shall be as Mount Zion, which cannot be removed, but abideth forever.' " And Johnny said, " Dear Mary, I wish I could see and feel as you do ; but I cannot. If God had not taken away our dear father, I think I could have borne my mother's death better. But, now both are gone, what shall we do?" — " Why, Johnny, do you not remember what dear father told us after mother's death? He said that his Saviour would be the orphans' God; and I am sure he will. And I want you to trust him now." — "Well, for your sake I will try."

Mr. Shields had ever been a very warm-hearted, consistent Christian man, whose counsel was ever sought because of his prudence and discretion. His life had been an open volume of love to God and good-will to men.

After the funeral the two orphans returned to their sad home. Mary said to Johnny, " I think we had better continue to keep house, and you do the farm-work, and I will help you all I can." Johnny assented to his dear sister's proposals. He had never thought of doing any thing without first submitting it to the judgment of his dear Mary; and his love for her since the death of his father had become, if possible, doubly intensified. He was so afraid something would happen to her when he was in the field at work, that he told her, if she ever wanted him, to blow the dinner-horn, and he would come to her at once. When the hay-season came on, he told his sister he would not be able to cut all their grass, cure it, and get it into the barn, without help; and Mary thought he ought to have help too. At this time a very good-looking young man asked Johnny if he knew of any person who wished to hire help through the hay-season ; and Johnny told him he wished to hire some one to help him get his hay. He agreed to work for Johnny for a dollar and fifty cents per day and his board, through the haying-season. Johnny invited him into the house, and introduced him to his sister Mary; and all went on very well until the third day, when Johnny missed his hired man, but thought nothing of it until he heard the well-known horn blow. Without dropping his pitchfork, he ran as quick as he could to the house. Mary appeared at one of the attic-windows, and told Johnny that the young man had insulted her, and she had taken the horn and fled to the attic, and fastened all the doors behind her, that she might be safe until he came.

Johnny, on hearing his sister's story, became so enraged,.that Mary was affrighted. She had never in her life seen her brother's temper raised before; and she began to beg him not to hurt the man, but pay him, and send him away. But Johnny would not listen to his sister now: she had been insulted, and that he would not for one moment bear. He would protect his sister with his life, if it was necessary. The man had fastened all the outside doors. He ordered him to open the door; but he refused. Johnny went into the cellar, and up the cellar-stairs; and in a moment he stood before the man who had insulted his dear sister Mary, with the following words: "I did not hire you to insult my sister. Now leave my house this moment. Come here to-morrow, and I will pay you what I owe you." The young man said, "You hired me for the hay-season, and I shall not leave until the season closes." Mary, hearing some loud words, and fearing the consequences, made her appearance, to aid, if possible, in the peaceable settlement of the matter. As soon as she came into the room, this young man attempted to embrace her in his arms. Johnny in an instant thrust his pitchfork through his body, and he fell to the floor with the cry, "You have killed me!" Johnny mounted a horse, and went for a physician, sending some of the neighbors to Mary's assistance. The doctor came, examined and dressed the wound, saying it was not dangerous; and the neighbors removed the man to the alms-house, to be cared for by the overseer. In the mean time, Johnny, fearing the consequences, told Mary he must flee, and leave, for fear of arrest. Mary besought him to give himself up to the officers of law, and all would be well. But Johnny was so filled with fear, that he dared not remain. Taking a few dollars and a few clothes, he very warmly embraced his dear sister, saying he would write to her, but would not tell her where he was going. It is doubtful if he knew himself where he was going; for he was so much excited, that he hardly knew what he did or said.

CHAPTER II.

YOUNG Shields made his way straight to a seaport, and found a ship bound to London, commanded by Capt. B——. After the ship had hauled into the stream he wrote to his sister.

Johnny was very seasick for a few days; and, after it was over, some of the old tars began to impose duties upon Johnny which he had never agreed to perform; and, if he showed the slightest indisposition to perform them, then they would strike and kick him. After patiently bearing their insults as long as ·he could, he told Capt. B—— how the crew had been treating him. Capt. B—— called all hands aft, and told them the first man that imposed upon his boy again he would put in irons for disobedience of orders. After this every thing went on quietly; and Johnny grew in favor with his captain and officers. Arriving in London, the second mate and all the crew left the ship. After the home cargo was in, and all stowed away, Capt. B—— called Johnny into the cabin, and said to him, "Although this is your first voyage, I am so well satisfied with your character, that I now offer you the the second officer's berth on board my ship; and Mr. Transom and myself will teach you all we can, and you must not be afraid or ashamed to ask any question of myself or of my first officer." Johnny was overwhelmed with astonishment at Capt. B——'s proposal; but he accepted the office, and filled it faithfully, to the satisfaction of both captain and mate.

They arrived home in 1850. He wrote to his sister to get some one to look after the place, and come and meet him at the T—— House. On the fifth day after his arrival his dear sister met him at the T—— House. After a warm, loving greeting, Mary wished him to return home with her. He then told her that he meant to follow the

sea, and hoped, by strict attention to his business, to rise
to a captain's office. She rejoiced with him in his promotion, and told him the man with whom he had the difficulty had got well, and had gone away to some other part
of the country. Mary spent only a few days with her
brother, and then returned to her country home. In
March her brother's ship sailed for San Francisco, with
fifty gold-hunting passengers on board, arriving there in
July. In August they sailed again for Hong Kong, where
they arrived after a passage of thirty-two days. In November they sailed for B——. All went on well till in
January. While scudding before a heavy gale, under a
close-reefed maintopsail and fore-staysail, through the
carelessness of the man at the wheel the ship broached
to ; and a sea swept overboard the man at the wheel, and
Mr. Transom the first officer, cleaning the decks of water-
casks, spare spars, and bulwarks, and making the ship
to tremble from truck to keelson. The captain and all
hands were on deck as soon as they could get there.
When it was found that Mr. Transom, the first officer,
had been swept overboard, a sad wail of woe was heard
by every man on board ; for he was loved by all, and by
none more than Johnny ; for he had been his teacher,
and Johnny had availed himself of his faithful instruc-
tions.

Capt. B—— mourned the loss of his first officer, who
had been with him several voyages, and expected to have
command of "The S——," or some other ship, on their
arrival home. Nothing more occurred worthy of note
during the remnant of their passage. But we must drop
the familiar term of Johnny now ; for he has become the
first officer of the noble ship "S——." They arrived the
following February, making the passage in one hundred
days from Hong Kong to B——.

After the cargo was discharged, Mr. Shields asked Capt.
B—— for a brief furlough, which was readily given. He
took the train for B——, and then hired a man to carry
him to his old home in G——. As he drew near, and
recognized some of the old trees, his heart leaped for joy
to think he should surprise his dear sister, and hold her
in his embrace ere she was aware. He arrived at the old

home about four P.M.; but, instead of meeting his dear sister Mary, he was met by a strange gentleman that he had never seen before. He immediately inquired for his sister, and made himself known as her brother, and was promptly told she was not at home. He inquired where she was; for he must see her, let her be wherever she might be. After a while the gentleman told him she was his wife, and had become insane, and he found it necessary to send her away because he could not live peaceably with her. Mr. Shields in a moment mistrusted that something was wrong; and, fearing he should arouse the man's suspicions, he assumed as quiet an appearance as possible. He then asked him when they were married. He told him on New-Year's Day, Jan. 1, 1851, and that their pastor, Rev. Mr. M——, had married them. Mr. Shields, being well acquainted with Mr. M——, thought it best to repair to the pastor's house to get a more correct solution of the strange story told him by his new-found brother-in-law. Mr. M—— gave him a warm and cordial reception, asking if he had been at his old home. After replying in the affirmative, Mr. M—— said, "Come into my study, and I will frankly tell you all I know about it. Mr. H—— came here to G—— some time in November last, and brought with him a letter from a church in New York, and upon that letter was received into our church. His zeal and apparent active piety made him many warm friends. He took charge of a Bible-class in our sabbath school; and his apparent ready knowledge of the Bible very soon won for him the admiration of all; and your dear sister Mary became very warmly attached to him. In December Mary came to me for advice, and I gave her as good counsel as I knew how to give. She said that Mr. H—— had asked her to become his wife. She kept nothing back. She told me what her father had said to her before he died; and like a loving, confiding girl, as she always was, she had come to her pastor for advice, and I freely gave it. While I could see no reason why she might not accept his proposals, yet, as he was an entire stranger, I could see nothing inconsistent with his waiting until she had more time and a better opportunity of judging his character. Before she left me I urged her

by all means to wait till your return. She thanked me
kindly for my counsel, but made me no other reply. I
soon became satisfied that he was pressing his suit with
such vigor that I feared the contract would soon be closed.
She never came to me for advice again. On the evening of last New-Year's Day they came to my house,
and I married them here. In three weeks after his marriage he was excluded from our church for gambling. I
suppose you knew your father left a thousand dollars in
the bank in B——; and her husband managed to get five
hundred dollars of that money, which was all spent in
gambling. Then Mary went to the bank, and forbade
them paying him any more money, saying the other five
hundred belonged to her brother. Finding that source
of income dry, he then entered the blacksmith's shop,
and carried all the tools away, and sold them for what he
could get. He then sold your father's family horse, and
spent the money in the same way; and it was some days
before his wife knew he had sold her horse. All these he
sold to gratify his gambling propensities. Only a few
days afterwards, one of her neighbors, Mr. D——, told
her that her husband had offered to sell him her favorite
cow Dolly for twenty dollars. She said to Mr. D——,
'I wish you to come here this evening as a witness to
what I wish to say to him.' That evening Mr. D——
came; and Mary said to him, in Mr. D——'s presence,·
'Mr. H——, you came here last fall, and brought a
letter from a B—— church in New York, and was cordially received; and at that time no member in the church
was more warmly loved than you were. Up to the time
you married me, last New-Year's Eve, you seemed to be
a consistent Christian man. Three weeks after our marriage you were excluded from the church for gambling;
and I tell you now, in the presence of Mr. D——, that
you are a base hypocrite. You have deceived me. Your
love for me was only assumed, that you might the better
accomplish your gambling designs, which at that time
were fully developed. You promised before God to love,
cherish, and protect me as your wife. Then I loved you,
and I did make sacrifices to gratify your wishes; but you
spent my money and sold my property without my knowl-

edge or consent. My father's horse, which had been one
of our family pets for several years, you sold without my
knowledge ; and last night you offered him my best cow,
dear old Dolly, for twenty dollars.' — ' If Mr. D——
says that, he. is a liar,' said the infuriated husband.
Mr. D—— then said, ' You came into my barn while I
was milking, and said you would sell me Dolly for twenty
dollars ; and I asked you if you had Mary's permission.
And do you not remember the reply you made me? " I
am master now, and will do with the property as I think
best." ' — ' Mr. D——, you are a liar, sir. I repeat it ;
and I wish you to leave my house at once.' Mr. D——
said, ' I will, but not till I have first taught you to carry
a civil tongue in your head.' And the sturdy farmer
took Mr. H—— by the collar, and cuffed his ears right
smartly, till he begged the farmer's pardon. Mr. D——
then left the house. As soon as he was gone, Mr. H——
laid hold of his wife, that he had promised to protect,
saying, ' I will pay you now for saying what you did in
Mr. D——'s presence.' He choked her until she fell ;
and, in falling, she struck her head violently upon the
stove. He then took her in his arms, and laid her upon
a bed ; for he was terribly frightened lest she would die.
He called to one of his neighbors to go for the doctor, and
it was some three hours before he came. He immediately
inquired about the cause ; and Mr. H—— said she fell
upon the stove, but said nothing about how she came to
fall upon the stove. The doctor, in his examination, discovered a large black spot upon each side of her neck,
which he could not seem to understand. Mrs. H——
was, after a long time, restored to consciousness ; but her
mind seemed to be wandering ; but she soon recognized
the doctor, and called him by name. Her husband came
to the bedside, intending to do something for her. She
said, ' Go away from me : you have killed me now.'
Then her mind seemed to wander again ; and then she
would cry, saying, ' Dear Lord, send my dear Johnny
home to me : Johnny will take care of me when he comes :
Johnny loves me, and I love Johnny.' The doctor told
Mr. H—— that it was necessary that some good woman
should take charge of Mrs. H——, and that she must be

kept very quiet. A little after, Mrs. H—— said to the doctor, ' I wish you would send for widow B—— to come and take care of me ; for she is a good Christian woman, but pray don't you leave me till she comes.'

" At this remark the doctor's suspicions were raised, whether those black spots were not caused by violence of some kind ; and he despatched one of the neighbors for widow B——. He had asked her husband to go ; but he refused, saying he might be needed in the house, but he never left the room while the doctor remained. Some two hours after, widow B—— came, and was very much astonished to find Mrs. H—— in such a condition. Widow B—— was a very smart, fearless woman, and a good Christian woman, and had heard of Mr. H——'s gambling proclivities. After she came, the doctor gave her directions, and went home, saying he would come again in the morning. Mr. H—— soon retired ; and, when he was gone, Mrs. H—— told widow B—— the whole story, how he choked her until she fell, and showed her the black spots he made upon her throat with his fingers. Widow B—— said to her that she had better say nothing to him now about the matter, and talk but little when he was in the room ; that she would take good care of her, and she should want for nothing.

" In the morning he came in, went to the bedside, and said, ' How are you feeling this morning? ' She said, ' My throat is very sore indeed.' He turned away at once, and showed evident signs of guilt. Through the day she showed evident signs of partial insanity at least. When the doctor came, and examined her, he shook his head, saying he had fears that she might lose her reason ; and several times, when she saw her husband, she would say, ' I hate him : drive him away. He sold my horse : he wants to kill me.' And she would cover herself up in the bedclothes to get out of his sight. Mr. H—— said to the doctor, ' Is it not strange that insane people often hate their best friends? ' The doctor replied, by saying it was strange ; but sometimes insane people knew who their best friends were. Nothing more was said upon this subject. Through the day she would at times seem to be filled with fear, and exclaim, ' Do save me from that man !

he means to kill me.' And then she would become as
quiet as an infant. Toward night she seemed more rational, and for the first time asked for food. The nurse
brought her some nice gruel ; and she drank it very freely,
and seemed more like herself than at any time since she
was taken sick. Through the night she slept quietly, and
in the morning she wanted to get up ; and she sat up the
most of the day, and seemed as rational as she ever was.
Her husband did not come into the room during the day.
The next day she went about the house some, and wished
to know if her cows were taken care of, and her fowls
and pigs. Mr. H—— suggested that she might now discharge her nurse, and save some expense. She replied,
saying it was a great pity that he did not think of saving
expense when he was gambling away her property. He
answered, saying, 'The least you say about that, the
better it will be for you.' The nurse coming in, nothing
more was said. He told the nurse she might go home in
the morning. She said that she should not leave as long
as Mrs. H—— wished her to remain. That morning the
doctor called in to see how she was getting along ; and
Mr. H—— asked the doctor if he was acquainted with
Dr. S——, the principal physician of the lunatic-asylum
at B——. He said he only knew him by repute, but
thought him very eminently fitted to fill that position. He
then asked the doctor if he did not think it would be a
good plan to request Dr. S—— to visit his wife, and for
him to meet with him in consultation : the doctor said he
certainly should have no objections. Mr. H—— said
he would write to him, and, when he received his reply,
would notify him of the time appointed for consultation. Two days afterward Dr. S—— came, and was introduced by the family physician to the nurse and to
Mrs. H——. She was surprised at seeing another physician called, without her being made aware of his coming ;
and it gave her nervous system such a sudden shock as to
dethrone her reason again for the time being. The consultation resulted in the opinions of the physicians that
she had better be removed to the asylum as soon as she
was able to be removed. Three days after the consultation, under a plea that a ride was prescribed by the physi-

cians, she was carried to the lunatic-asylum in B——, and she has now been there two weeks. Thus I believe I have given you every item concerning your sister Mary, as far as I have known them, since her marriage to Mr. H——."

Mr. Shields then said, "My dear sister Mary, your imprisonment in B—— and to that man will soon terminate." The next morning he called upon their family physician, and said, "I wish you to go with me to B—— to aid me in procuring the liberty of my sister from her tyrannical captivity." Arriving at the asylum, Mr. Shields was introduced to Dr. S——, the principal physician, as Mrs. H——'s only brother. On his inquiring after the health of his sister, the doctor said he did not see but she was as rational as any person he ever saw. Mr. Shields said, "Doctor, I wish to see her at once." The doctor said, "It may be too much for her, and bring on a relapse." Mr. Shields said he had no fears for the result. The doctor then said Mr. H——, her husband, did not wish him to allow any person to see her without his written permission. Mr. Shields then said, "Doctor, I shall not ask the permission of a hypocrite or thief to see my own dear sister, that he has deceived, insulted, and abused. Doctor, you will lead me to her at once, or order some other person to show me to her room."

The doctor, on hearing these statements, immediately went with him. The moment the door opened, and she saw her brother, she exclaimed, "Dear Saviour, I expected an answer to my prayers;" and then, throwing her arms around her brother's neck, she wept like a child, and seemed unwilling to leave him for a single moment. Finally, after her outburst of joy, she said, "You have come to take me away, and to save me from future cruelties from my husband." Her brother merely said, "We will not discuss that matter now. I will take care of you, and take care of your husband too." She gathered up her things, entered the carriage, rode back to G——, and drove right to the parsonage, where they were received with the warmest affection.

Mr. Shields then said, "I have already been detained from my business longer than I expected; but I have a little more business to do before I leave, and shall begin right now.'' Turning to his sister, he said, '' Do you not wish to be divorced from your husband?'' She answered, '' Yes, I do. Though I do not believe in divorces as a general thing, I think my circumstances will justify it.''

Mr. Shields found no difficulty in procuring her divorce, with such testimony as that of Rev. Mr. Merritt, widow B——, Mr. D——, and their family physician. The husband was called to show any reasons why the divorce should not be made; but his guilt prevented him from putting in an appearance at the trial; and the divorce was granted. Mr. Shields then went to his old home, and showed Mr. H—— the divorce-papers, and told him that he did not wish to have any trouble with him, that he would give him twenty-four hours to gather together whatever property was really his own, and leave the place, or he would sue him for gambling away the property of her who once was his wife, but never would be again. Mr. H—— asked Mr. Shields if he could not be permitted to see Mrs. H—— for a few moments before he left; and he told him, ''Never! She has suffered enough from you already, and she never wishes to see you again.'' The next day Mr. Shields hired the farm to a young farmer just married. He did not think it prudent for his sister to live there alone; and she remained at Mr. Merritt's, their pastor, her brother being responsible for her board.

CHAPTER III.

MR. SHIELDS having finished up all his business, and placed his sister in a respectable Christian home, returned to B——, where he found the ship all loaded, and ready for sea. Capt. B—— informed Mr. Shields that Mr. L——, his owner, and his only child and daughter Alice, would take passage with them to Liverpool, and then they were going on a Continental tour. Mr. L—— was a very wealthy man : he had lost his very amiable wife about one year before, and he had not felt like doing business since, and thought that rest and travel would be an advantage to himself and daughter.

They sailed in May, 1851. On the second day after sailing, the wind from the eastward, with a heavy head-beat sea, and the ship under double-reefed topsails, not making over three miles per hour, Miss Alice came out upon deck, walked to the lee-side, near where Mr. Shields was standing, very sea-sick indeed, and her father had told her she would feel better upon deck. She began vomiting over the side of the ship ; and the ship suddenly gave what sailors call a heavy lurch and a deep roll at the same time. Alice, losing her foothold, was in a moment plunged head-foremost into the sea. Mr. Shields sent an order from his iron lungs that was heard by all below as well as all upon deck : "Throw the main and mizzen topsails aback ! " And he seized the end of a long coil of rope, and then leaped into the sea, and, seizing the affrighted girl, said, " *Do not fear: I will save you.*" In a few moments the men pulled them both alongside ; and in a few moments more both were safely landed upon deck. The young lady was carried into the cabin ; and dry clothes and an hour's rest fully restored her, and cured her sea-sickness. She went to Mr. Shields, and presented him with a large, beautiful gold locket, with the following accompanying note : " Mr. Shields, my dear sir, please accept this locket at the hand of the donor, not as payment for saving my life, but as a token of my esteem for such daring, unparalleled bravery. Perhaps, if life is spared, a more satisfactory sacrifice may be made at some future day. From your loving friend, with ever grateful remembrance, *Alice L.*"

Mr. Shields was much affected with the gift and the note, and said, in reply, that he only did his duty; while he felt very grateful for the gift she had bestowed. He put them both away together. At the time, he did not even open the locket to see its contents.

Mr. L——, her father, said to Mr. Shields, "You have saved the life of my only child ; and my gratitude I never can express to you in language, and shall not attempt it. But rest assured, my dear sir, that you have bound obligations upon me that this life will not be long enough to discharge. You will ever be held by my daughter and myself in grateful remembrance." Mr. Shields said in reply, " Mr. L——, please receive my sincere thanks for your gratitude and good wishes ; but, sir, I should have made the attempt to save your daughter Alice if I had known my own life would be forfeited to save hers." Almost every pleasant evening during their passage to Liverpool was Mr. Shields seen walking the quarter-deck, with the trusting Alice hanging upon his strong arm. This mutual, trusting confidence was witnessed by her father with evident delight. He had told Capt. B—— that he hoped that Alice would press her suit; for it would be the proudest moment of his life to give his Alice into the keeping of such a man as Mr. Shields. Capt. B—— said he had been with him, from a green hand right from the country, up to this time, and a more noble specimen of manhood he had never seen ; and, if he had a marriageable daughter, he had never seen a man to whom he would so soon confide her as to Mr. Shields for a husband.

They arrived safely in Liverpool; and Alice and her father, after an affectionate leave-taking, took the train for London. They remained only one week in London, and then left for Paris ; but, before leaving, Alice wrote to Mr. Shields. As we did not see that letter, we shall not attempt to describe its contents.

Before he sailed, Mr. Shields received a letter from his sister Mary, announcing the death of his pastor's wife. Mary said she took care of her while she was sick, and that she died as she had lived, in triumphant faith and love : her end was peace and joy. Mr. Merritt had requested her to remain, and keep his house, and take care of his only little son but two years of age, and she had consented so to do ; and, instead of having to pay her board, she could earn something for herself.

After discharging their cargo, and taking in another, they sailed for New York, where they arrived safely in September, 1851. Mr. Shields spent one week only with his sister, and returned to New York, where he found a letter awaiting him from Alice L——. She and her father were then in Rome. He immediately replied to her letter, directing it to Naples, according to her direction. The ship was soon laden with her cargo, bound to Rio Janeiro. Mr. Shields felt somewhat disappointed. He had hoped they would go to some part of Europe, that he might be nearer to the idol of his affections. They sailed in November, 1851, arriving safely there early in January, 1852. Just before they sailed for New York, he received a letter from Alice's father, saying that Alice's health was so poor, he thought it best to return home, that she might have more suitable medical advice, and said he hoped to be in B—— by the first of April. They were so soon to leave, that Mr. Shields could not reply to this letter, but hoped all would be well. He sailed for New York the first of February, 1852. All prospered well, and Mr. Shields thought they should have a short passage home. But in crossing the Gulf Stream, not far from Cape Hatteras, they suddenly encountered a terrible thunder-storm ; and about midnight they experienced a tremendous crash of thunder and lightning, which threw every man upon deck. When the terrible crash subsided, they found their mainmast and mizzenmast both gone, having been carried away by the lightning (which struck them), and shivered into a hundred pieces. No man, however, was killed ; but all the watch upon deck had been so stunned by the stroke, that several hours elapsed before they were restored to consciousness. Mr. Shields was below at the time the lightning struck the ship, but was upon deck with Capt. B—— in a moment afterwards.

They could do but little towards clearing away the wreck of broken spars and rigging, until daylight made its appearance. They then fitted and rigged two jury-masts out of the broken spars, and put all the sail upon them they could, and stood in for the land. When in sight of Cape Henry, they signalized a steamer, which took them in tow, and towed them into New York, where they arrived safely after a passage of seventy-four days.

Mr. Shields found a letter for him from Mr. L——, wishing him to come to B—— immediately on his arrival. He showed his letter to Capt. B——, who released him, and bade him go at once. He immediately left for B——, where he arrived the next morning, and repaired at once to Mr. L——'s house. The servant ushered him into the parlor, and went to announce the name of the guest. Mr. L—— gave Mr. Shields a very cordial greeting, and said their physician had forbidden any person, except the father and nurse, seeing Alice. Mr. Shields replied by saying, "This quarantine will be pretty hard for me to bear. I do not wish nor intend to break through your physician's regulations; but I think my presence will do more for Alice's recovery than all the physicians in B——. I come to this conclusion by the last letter I received from her."

While they were talking, the doctor came in. Mr. Shields was introduced, and he at once stated to him his convictions; and it was thought best, finally, that Mr. Shields should be permitted to enter the sick-room. As soon as he stood inside of her room, and she saw him, she exclaimed, "My ever dear Johnny! You saved my life once before, and now you have come to save me a second time." She called him to her bedside, threw her arms around his neck, and held him for some moments in her embrace. She then said, "Dear father, do not let my Johnny ever leave me again." Suffice it to say, that Alice began to grow stronger every day; but she could not bear that he should be out of her room hardly a moment, fearing he would again go to sea without her. Alice made rapid strides in recovering from her sickness after Mr. Shields's return; and by the middle of May she had so far recovered as to ride out with the dear sailor, as she sometimes called him who had jeopardized his own life to save hers. She said to him that she thought the beautiful month of June, when mountain, hill, plain, and valley were all clothed with their garniture of summer beauty and flowers, was the most fitting time for their marriage. Mr. Shields said he had no objections; but he wished to visit his sister, and bring her back with him to witness the marriage-ceremony. Alice not only gave her consent, but was very anxious to meet her who was so soon to be her sister. She remarked to Mr. Shields, "If she is only one-half as good as you, I think I shall love her almost as much as I do you, for I never had a sister."

The next morning Mr. Shields left B—— for G——; and the meeting of brother and sister was like that of days and years gone by. Mr. Shields soon made known the principal object of his visit; and he noticed that Mary seemed somewhat confused and embarrassed, and he could not seem to understand the cause. But she soon said, "My dear brother, as I have never kept any secrets from you, I will not now. Mr. Merritt, for whom I have kept house since the death of his wife, has made proposals to me to become his wife, and I have not yet assented; and I am so glad you have come, that I may have your counsel and advice in the matter." Her brother said he knew of no reason why she should not accept his offer at once. "If you will accept his proposal, I should like to have a hand in the arrangement."

Mary at once accepted the Rev. Mr. Merritt's proposal; and her brother then said to Mr. Merritt, "You need some relaxation from your labors; and I now propose that you and Mary go with me to B——, and that we both be married at the same time. I know it will be very gratifying to my dear Alice and to her father likewise." They both cheerfully complied with their brother's wishes. Mr. Shields then wrote to Alice, stating the whole matter to her, which filled her soul, as it were, with ecstatic joy.

Two days after, Mr. Merritt, with Mary and the little

boy, who had for some time been calling her mother, with Mr. Shields, left for B——. The object of the pastor's absence was known, and approved by all the members of his church that knew about it.

They all arrived safely in B——, and were received with that open, frank cordiality which ever characterizes the wealthy merchants of B——. Alice fell in love with Mary at first sight ; and Mary gave her such a warm, cordial, sisterly embrace, that one would have thought they were old friends, instead of meeting each other for the first time. Mr. Merritt won the love of all hearts by his love, and kind Christian spirit, which were so distinctly seen by all present. As the hour for retiring drew near, Mr. Merritt said to Mr. L——, " I have for years been accustomed to maintain daily worship in my family at home, and, when abroad among strangers, to ask their permission and ask them to join with me if they wish." Mr. L—— at once said, " We all believe in the powerful efficacy of prayer, and shall most cordially unite with you, not in form only, but, I trust, with all our hearts." They all knelt together, after reading the Scriptures ; and Mr. Merritt poured out of his trusting soul a petition to Jesus for his wisdom to guide them all through the remnant of their earthly pilgrimage. Then he asked God, with a trembling voice, to bless and sanction his own marriage to his beloved Mary, who had been such a faithful tower of strength to him in his late bereavement ; and then he fervently prayed that Mr. Shields, in his union to Alice, might not forget the necessity of his more important union to Jesus, —that an indwelling Jesus alone could render the conjugal relation a peaceful, prosperous, and happy one. He closed by reminding him of his dying mother's counsel to him when a mere boy. When they arose from their knees, all had been deeply affected, even to tears ; and Mr. Shields was evidently much affected. He who could brave old ocean's storms amid its intensest fury, he who could plunge into the ocean to save another from drowning, did not, on this never-to-be-forgotten evening, forget the words of his dying mother: " *My prayers will be answered. God will save you, my dear boy.*" Never in all his life did those words come home to his soul with such mighty power.

After the good-night had been given by each, they all retired to seek repose, and fit them for the duties of the expected morrow. Mr. Shields also retired to his room, but not until he had sought his beloved Alice and his sister Mary, and besought them to pray for him. Neither Alice nor Mary took off their clothes until the clock had struck the third hour of morning, when each felt and believed their prayers had been answered, because all their anxiety for the one they loved had been removed. They then both went to bed, and slept in perfect peace and quietude until the clock striking eight awakened them from their slumbers; and trusting Mary said to Alice, "This will be the happiest morning for you and me that we have ever known." Alice's faith was not quite as strong as Mary's. But let us look into the sacred enclosure of Mr. Shields's room. There we may see him on his knees, with his open Bible in the chair where he knelt. He evidently had been studying the fifty-first psalm; and he found his case to be like that of David. There he read, meditated, and prayed, until the light broke in upon his mind, and he felt a sweet peace and joy he had never known before. He at first hardly dared to sleep, fearing he should not feel as he did before he lay down upon his bed; but he soon fell asleep, and dreamed that he saw his mother and father both rejoicing over his salvation. He did not believe much in dreams, and never spake of it till many years afterwards.

In the morning, when he first awoke, he felt of all men on earth he certainly was among the happiest, if not the most happy. Mary and Alice were so impatient, they could hardly wait his appearance in the drawing-room below. They soon heard him coming, and they both bounded toward him with that trusting love which did not wait for any expression from his lips; for that sweet, placid smile which so completely overspread his manly face told the story more positively than a thousand tongues. He finally said, "I understand now that psalm which says, 'He brought me up also out of a horrible pit, out of the miry clay, and set my feet upon a rock, and established my goings; and he hath put a new song in my mouth, even praise unto our God. Many shall see it and fear, and shall trust in the Lord.' That, I trust, has been my experience during the past night." Mr. L——, and his former pastor, Mr. Merritt, rejoiced with him in his new-found Saviour's love. As soon as the breakfast was past, a hymn was sung, accompanied by the organ played by Alice, and they knelt together. Mr. Merritt led in a fervent prayer of thanksgiving to their prayer-answering Saviour ; and, as soon as he had added the amen to his petition, Mr. Shields broke out in thanksgiving to Jesus, who had taken away the sins of his life, and given him an assured evidence of his acceptance through Jesus Christ.

The parlor was then cleared of every thing movable but the large sofa and organ ; and the few invited guests began to assemble in the drawing-room. The two sisters assisted each other in dressing for the bridal altar. The only invited guests were Mr. L——'s partner in business, Capt. B——, and Mr. L——'s sister and her husband. Mr. Merritt, at eleven A.M., walked into the parlor with Mary clinging to his arm ; and they took their places according to their mutual arrangament as bride and groom. Mr. Shields and Alice followed after them, filling the place of bride's man and maid until they were made one by the officiating clergyman. Then they, in turn, took the same places that had been filled by Mr. Shields and Alice, who were soon made husband and wife ; and the clergyman playfully remarked that Mrs. Shields would never have any regret in confiding herself to the love and care of a man who had jeopardized his own life to save her from a watery grave. Mr. Shields replied that he did not mean she ever should regret ; and Alice said she apprehended no danger in that direction.

After the wedding-hymn was sung, — composed for the occasion, and which will be found on the last page of this book, — they repaired to the dining-room, where a costly meal awaited their craving appetites ; and, after supplying all the necessities of the inner man, the guests all retired, and Mr. Merritt invited Mr. Shields and his bride to return with them to their country home in Vermont. Alice seemed delighted with spending a few days with her dear sister Mary. There were but three years difference in their ages ; Alice being three years younger than Mary, and but one year younger than her husband. The next morning they took the train for B——. On their way Mary told her sister she must not expect to find the quantity and the quality of comforts that she found in her father's home. Alice, in reply, said, "If I only have your society, my only dear sister, it is enough. Remember, I am used to travelling ; and, instead of complaining, I expect to receive some profitable lessons in housekeeping, which I very much need. At noon, or soon after, they arrived at B—— ; and Alice was delighted with all the scenery, and especially the rushing stream of the old Connecticut River. They all dined at B——, and hired a private conveyance to G——, where they arrived about four P.M.

Mary very soon donned her working-dress, and went to work to prepare their evening meal. As soon as it was found that their pastor had come, several of the sisters of the church came to Mary's assistance. Mary introduced them to her brother and sister, and Alice was delighted with them. Supper was soon prepared by Mary and her efficient helpers. That evening was their weekly prayer-meeting night, and all attended the meeting ; and it was one that will not soon be forgotten by that people. After their pastor had opened the meeting, and made a few brief remarks, Mr. Shields arose, and said, "This is the first regular prayer-meeting I have attended for several years. I have, in days gone by, been known to many that I see here to-night ; but I arise to tell you I am but two days old." And when he told them of his night's struggle with his sins, and of the joys of pardoned sin, there were but few dry eyes in that assembly. As soon as he sat down, Alice arose, and said, "You are all strangers to me, but I trust not to my Saviour, who has more than answered my prayers and my dear sister Mary's. While he who is now my dear husband was absent on his last voyage, my love could not seem to wait for his return, and I fell into a state of despondency. I then felt, if his life could only be spared, and I could see him once more, for which I most earnestly prayed, that I should be satisfied ; and God has not only answered my prayers in returning him to me, but answered our united prayers for his salvation ; so that to-night I believe I am one of the happiest women upon earth.'' Mary said she was enjoying very much of Jesus' love, and rejoiced with her brother in his new relations both temporally and spiritually. Several others took part in the exercises of the hour. The pastor then closed the meeting with the benediction ; and, after a general introduction and hand-shaking, they separated for their respective homes.

CHAPTER IV.

MR. SHIELDS and wife spent a week with Mary and her husband. The following sabbath morn was indeed beautiful : mountain, hill, and valley were dressed in living green ; and the wild as well as the cultivated flowers seemed to vie with the trusting, loving hearts which were glowing with that ardent Christian love to God and man which makes it in some measure resemble heaven. After the morning devotions all sought their rooms to seek a preparation of heart for enjoying the services of the sanctuary. Very soon the church-bell sent its gladdening tones of music through the valleys, calling its worshippers to God's temple for worship. There was an unusually large congregation present ; for their loved pastor had been absent, and each one longed to see his sweet face again, and give him a cordial welcome to their hearts. As the bell was striking its last tolling notes, Mr. Merritt entered, with his newly-married wife upon his arm, whom they all well knew and tenderly loved, followed by Mr. Shields and his wife. The whole congregation arose, and remained standing till the party were seated, as a token of love and respect for their pastor. The choir, led by the organ, then sung a hymn of welcome. Mr. Merritt read the Scriptures, and offered an importunate prayer for divine aid, and for God's blessing upon the service of the hour.

After singing, Mr. Merritt arose, and in a mild but clear voice announced his text in Prov. xi. 24 : "There is that scattereth, and yet increaseth ; and there is that withholdeth more than is meet, but it tendeth to *poverty*." He said the great principle found in the text was, that every thing in heaven and earth and in the sea was only increased by scattering. "God," he says, "acts upon this principle : God scatters light, that it may increase.

God scatters love, that love may increase. Every flower, tree, vine, and shrub, all scatter their seed to increase their species. And you as farmers know how hard you have to labor to keep the pernicious weeds from scattering their poisonous seed upon your farms. This morning God sends us all to these varied things, to learn a rich lesson," which he hoped to see reduced to daily practice. We have neither time nor room for any thing more than a brief synopsis of this truly excellent practical sermon. He said God had, at an infinite expense, provided means for breaking up and cleansing the garden of the human heart, that it might produce a rich harvest of fruit to his glory, and then scatter the seeds of holy living by a consistent Christian example at all times and in all places. He then spoke of the mighty power of our influence over the minds of others. He then said the husband and father have influence over their children; the mother and wife have that influence; and woe betide the mothers of this generation if they fail to scatter Jesus' love into the hearts of their children! Again he said, "My dear hearers, you will scatter seed, whether you intend it or not."

We wish we could give our readers the whole of this sermon; but we cannot now. Just a few words of his explanation of the latter part of his text: "And there is that withholdeth more than is meet; but it tendeth to *poverty*." "Is there a parent here to-day," he said, "that will withhold a peaceful, useful life, and a glorious victor's death, and an unfading crown of glory, from husband, wife, child, neighbor, or friend? Do you not know, that by withholding your prayers, your personal conversation with them in regard to their salvation, you will impoverish that soul forever? Can any of you to-day measure the depth of that poverty which will overwhelm all those who are found upon the left hand of Jesus, the Judge of quick and dead, when he shall come the second time to save, acquit, and bless all those who love him, and to punish his unbelieving enemies?"

He then closed by urging, with all the love and pathos of his own burdened soul, the vast importance of using all our time, talents, money, and influence in scattering

the good seed which Jesus had purchased in the garden
of bloody sweat and agony, as well as at Calvary, where
he bore our sins in his own body on the tree, that we,
being dead to sins, should live unto righteousness, by
whose stripes ye were healed. "Dearly beloved, as you
go from this temple to-day, take with you for your encour-
agement these most precious promises : ' In the morning
sow thy seed, and in the evening withhold not thy hand ;
for thou knowest not which will prosper, either this or
that, or whether they shall be alike *good*. Blessed are
ye that sow beside all *waters*.' ' Sow to yourselves in
righteousness, reap in mercy, break up your fallow
ground ; for it is time to seek the Lord till he come and
rain righteousness upon *you*, for he that goeth forth and
weepeth, bearing precious seed, shall doubtless return
again with rejoicing, bringing his sheaves with *him*.' "
He then, in a few well-chosen words, urged the impeni-
tent sinner that moment to sow to the Spirit, that he might
reap everlasting life ; and he then repeated the last warning uttered by John Baptist : " He that believeth on the
Son hath everlasting life ; and he that believeth not the
Son shall not see life, but the wrath of God abideth on
him." The Doxology was sung by the whole congregation standing, and the benediction given ; and all dis-
persed to meditate upon the solemn, impressive truths to
which they had listened.

  In the afternoon he gave them another excellent sermon. His subject was the power of the living Christian's
example. The word of his text was, " The path of the
just is as the shining light, that shineth more and more
until the perfect day." This, like his morning discourse,
was full of warning, instruction, entreaty, and comfort.
In the evening they had an excellent prayer-meeting, in
which Mr. Shields said he had received some excellent
instruction, and that he meant to reduce it to daily practice during the rest of his future life. We shall see,
ere long, how well he carried his consistent resolution into
practice.

  Mr. Shields and his wife remained a few more days at
the parsonage with their brother and sister ; and little
Georgie cried sadly when dear aunt Alice and uncle

John came to leave for their home. They both were very much pleased with their visit; and on Tuesday one of the brethren volunteered his services to carry them to B——, where they took the train for B——. Mr. L—— was not at home when his children came; but he came home shortly afterwards, and, after giving them a loving father's joyous greeting, said it seemed to him as though they had been gone a month, instead of only a single week. After tea he said, "John, I have to-day contracted for the building of a new ship for you in Bath; and I wish you to go there, and superintend her while building, and see that no green or improper timber is put into her frame." He replied by saying he would assume the responsibility with one single provision, and that was, that his Alice must go with him. His father said, "I expected that, of course; and, when I gave you my dear Alice, it was a life-lease that I gave you of her." Alice said, "I love you, my dear father; but I could not live away from my idolized Johnny." Mr. Shields said, "Do not say that, my dear Alice. Remember our dear brother Merritt's advice, that all our love in this world must be always subordinated to the claims of Jesus our dear Saviour." — "You are right, as you always are, my dear Johnny; and I will endeavor to speak more guarded in the future." — "That is right, Alice dear. A frank, open confession of our faults will do us good; and I only hope I shall always be as ready to confess my own faults as you have now been."

Mr. L—— said it would not be necessary for them to go for some weeks yet; for they had not yet begun to haul the timber into the yard. He then said to his son, "Capt. B—— sailed yesterday for Cronstadt, Russia; and Mr. Bell, who was your second mate, has gone as his first officer." Mr. Shields said he was a good, practical seaman, and in every respect a worthy man.

He then said to his father, "Did you know that Capt. B—— is not a Christian man?" He said, "Yes. I have had many conversations with him; but he always had so many excuses, that I could never make any permanent impression upon his mind." Johnny said, "Oh, if I could only have seen him before he sailed! I think

he would have been influenced by me when I told him how
I found Jesus, or, rather, how and where Jesus found
me." Alice playfully said, "Johnny dear, if you think
you can have such power over men, I shall begin to think
you had better leave your seafaring life, and study for the
ministry." — "Well, dear Alice, do you think that none
but ministers can scatter the golden seed of gospel truth?
I am sure I never shall forget the pointed, practical truths
embodied in that sermon which our dear brother Merritt
preached last sabbath." — "Neither shall I, dear Johnny.
I think it one of the best sermons I ever heard. He has
talents and ability of a rare character. I confess I was
very much surprised."

The two happy children spent some four weeks at
home, making their dear father as happy as they were
themselves. And, when they had all packed ready for
going, their father said, "I shall expect to see you home
every Saturday night to spend the sabbath with me."
They went immediately to Bath, and hired suitable rooms,
where they could be alone whenever they chose. When
Mr. Shields arrived, he gave his letter of introduction to
the master-builder, who, after reading his letter of instruc-
tions, said, "Then you have come to show me how to
build a ship, have you?" Mr. Shields said that was not
his business; but, as he was to command the ship when
she was completed, he was there to see that no shoddy
timber was put into her frame; that he knew his business,
and proposed to attend to it in the interest of his owner,
whose agent he was. The master-builder, finding that
Capt. Shields was not to be easily moved from his pur-
pose, ever after treated him with respect and esteem.

In September, the time of launching being near, a
name for the new ship was to be considered; and Capt.
Shields wished to have her called Alice, after his wife.
But she preferred the name of Mary Alice; and her
father and husband both gave way to Alice. She then
said, "Did Mary ever see a ship launched?" And
Johnny said, "They neither build nor launch ships in
Vermont, where she has spent her life." Alice proposed
that she and her husband be invited to come and with her
launch in their new and future home. Accordingly an

invitation was sent; and, as neither of them had ever been on board of a ship, they accepted the invitation. On the third day after, they arrived in B——. The next day being the highest tide at twelve M., she was to be set afloat to commence her life's history; for ships, as well as men and women, have a history.

Alice and Mary stood upon the topgallant forecastle; and, as the last shore was removed, she began to glide down the ways, increasing her velocity till she rolled out large volumes of smoke from her ways. As she touched the water, Alice exclaimed as loud as she could, standing beside her dear sister Mary, "I now name this sea-going traveller 'The Mary Alice' of B——." She glided for the first time into what was to be her future element with great rapidity and safety.

She was soon hauled in to the wharf to receive her masts, rigging, and sails. After the masts were put into their place, Mr. L—— thought best to have her towed by a steamer to B—— to complete her outfit: so he might have his children with him as much as it was possible before they went to sea. Mr. Merritt and wife remained, and came with them to B—— in the new ship. They were both delighted; neither of them having ever been on board of a ship or upon the ocean before. They arrived safely in B——, being only one night upon the ocean. Mr. Merritt said he had found timber enough in that short voyage for a dozen sermons.

The next day they were obliged to leave for their mountain home, which they did, after making promises of writing, &c. Capt. Shields then said, "My dear brother and sister, you are about to leave us, and we may never meet again until we meet with Jesus and his redeemed on the other side of the river of death. Pray for 'The Mary Alice,' and pray for me, that I may carry into execution my resolutions which were the outgrowth of your sermon upon scattering; for, God being my helper, I mean to scatter his truth during the remnant of my days, wherever God in his providence may cast my lot in life; for I never can be forgetful or ungrateful towards that Saviour who plucked me as a brand from the burning when I had well-nigh consumed myself by my own guilty sins."

The good wishes and good-bys were spoken, and they departed. In a few days the new ship "Mary Alice" was advertised as ready for freight, and would take a few cabin-passengers for San Francisco, commanded by Capt. John Shields. Alice had engaged for a maid a good Christian girl, by the name of Annie Baker. She had been engaged as a sewing-girl. She came from Vermont; but more of her will be seen in the future. On the 1st of November, 1854, the whole number on board was thirty-six, consisting of the captain, his wife and maid, three mates, cook, steward and stewardess, and carpenter, and twenty-two men before the mast. They experienced but little rough weather. The first night after sailing, Capt. Shields ordered his first officer, Mr. Helm, to call all hands aft upon the quarter-deck. He then said to them, "I am a Christian man, and my wife is a Christian woman; and at four bells (six P.M.) I expect all hands — except the officer of the deck, the man at the wheel, and the man at the lookout — to come aft into the house to attend our daily prayer-meeting. We all have souls, and but one short, uncertain life to secure their salvation in. Men, obey your officers, do your duty faithfully, and you will find in me a constant friend that will do every thing to contribute to your comfort. You may all now go forward to your duties."

Although the passengers were sick at first, the next day, at four bells (six o'clock), all came aft, but one gentleman and his wife, who remained outside upon deck. Alice began singing, "Guide me, O thou great Jehovah!" The first officer had charge of the deck. The second and third officers proved to be excellent singers; and some four or five of the men could sing nicely. After singing, Capt. Shields read a portion of Scripture, and then said, "I do not command you to kneel with me; but it would be very pleasing to me if you would all kneel before the Lord our Maker." In a moment every one of them was upon their knees: Capt. Shields then poured out his full soul to God for his guidance and protection, and prayed earnestly that he would convert and save all on board. The amen was no sooner uttered than the gentleman passenger, Mr. G——, prayed most fervently; and, when he had done, an old tar by the name of Jack said, "Capt. Shields, may I pray, sir?" The captain said, "Yes, pray on." And Jack Carter offered such a prayer that all hearts were melted, and Alice wept like a child. The hour having expired, he said, "Men, you will all be better fitted for this season of prayer." Jack Carter said Jesus had been his Saviour for many years, and he was glad to get on board of a ship where Jesus' claims were respected.

The gentleman apologized to Capt. Shields at the breakfast-table next morning, saying that he and his wife were both members of a Methodist church in L——; but their religion at the present seemed to be nothing but a mere form, and hoped he would remember them in their prayers. This they all promised to do. Alice, having received a splendid musical education, suggested she should like very much to teach or give any lessons in singing to any that wished to learn; and both of the gentlemen and their wives said they loved singing, but they knew nothing about the notes, or rules of singing. So every pleasant day — and they had many of them while passing between the tropics — Alice would gather her club on deck when it was pleasant, at other times in the house, or cabin.

With fair winds "The Mary Alice" was making rapid progress. Mr. Helm, the first officer, said he never had seen a ship before that could run off ten knots from the reel on a bowline; and this "The Mary Alice" had done during the last twenty-four hours. Alice and the passengers all said they had never seen any thing in their lives that equalled the magnificent beauty of the tropical sunsets. Their beauty cannot be described: they must be seen in order to be appreciated.

One day a large shoal of porpoises came pitching and playing round the bows of their ship. The second mate plunged a harpoon into one of them, and in a few moments it was upon deck, bleeding from the wound made by the harpoon. The blubber, which covers their entire bodies, was soon stripped off; and the meat, which resembles venison, was hung up in long strips to dry it upon the outside. By so doing it may be preserved for many days. But the meat of a single porpoise, although it weighed a hundred and twenty pounds, would not furnish many meals for thirty people.

The sabbath broke in upon them with all its tropical splendor; and Capt. Shields gave orders for every man to don his best suit, and all work to be suspended, and at four bells (ten A.M.) all hands to come aft, upon the quarter-deck, for their sabbath-morning worship. At the appointed hour every man put in his appearance according to orders; and all that could sing meeting together under Alice's training, had become a very efficient choir. Capt. Shields read that beautiful old hymn, "Thus far the Lord hath led me on," &c. Ten of them could sing; and Alice said, "We will sing 'Old Hundred.'" When those ten voices unitedly pealed forth those precious words, every heart was so much affected as to moisten the eyes of all present. After singing, Capt. Shields said, "Let us unitedly ask God's blessing upon this morning hour of worship; and as he knelt every other knee bent, some of them, doubtless, out of respect to their commander, and others out of love and respect to Jesus, who had saved them from their guilty sins. Capt. Shields loved to pray; and this morning he seemed to be exercised with the crushing weight of responsibility which rested upon him. While he confessed his own unworthiness and weakness, yet in his prayer you could see childlike and implicit trust in Jesus for all that he asked. He most fervently prayed God to save all the sons of the ocean; but in an especial manner did he plead with his heavenly Father to lead to Jesus, and save, every member of his ship's company. After prayer he read and explained, with all the ability God had given him, the parable of the "prodigal son." He related his own personal experience in connection with his remarks; and when he told of his midnight struggles with his own guilty sins, and of his wife and sister spending almost a whole night in prayer to God for his salvation, several of his sailors sobbed aloud, and every heart was, for the time at least, melted and subdued. Several others spoke of the love they had for Jesus, with the reasons why they loved him. They sang a few more hymns, and were dismissed.

A few moments only had elapsed when the man on the lookout exclaimed, "Sail ho!" — "Where away?" was the inquiry of the officer on watch. "Two points oft the lee-bow, sir." A report was made to Capt. Shields, and he ordered his ship kept off two points to intercept the strange ship. In less than an hour the stranger hauled up his courses, and backed his maintopsail, waiting the approach of "The Mary Alice." Capt. Shields ordered the fore and main courses hauled up, topgallant-sails clewed down, and, trumpet in hand, exclaimed, "What ship is that, pray?" The stranger replied, "'The Comet,' from Rio Janeiro, bound for New York; J. W—— master." The stranger then asked, "What ship is that?" And the captain replied, "'The Mary Alice' of B——; eighteen days out; bound to San Francisco; commanded by John Shields. I wish you to report all well on board on your arrival." The trumpet of the stranger was waved only in reply. All sail was again crowded upon "The Mary Alice," and she was soon moving through the watery element with majestic grandeur and rapidity.

That night in their meeting, one of the men, by the name of Bill Swan, said, "I want to be a Christian man, like Jack Carter and my captain; and I wonder if anybody on board loves my poor soul enough to pray for me as our captain's wife had prayed for him." Alice arose amid her tears, and said, "One soul is just as precious in Jesus' sight as another." And she told him, if he would pray for himself till Jesus forgave his sins, as his captain had done, she would pray all night for his salvation. He replied, saying he would; for he felt that he was one of the greatest sinners upon the ocean. Annie, Alice's maid, said she would pray with her mistress for him too; and then the two lady-passengers said they would join with them.

At one o'clock A.M. Bill Swan came to the second mate, who was officer of the watch, and said, "I wish you would tell the captain's wife she need not pray any more for me; for about half an hour ago there was such a load tumbled off of my soul, that I know something has been done, and if it ain't religion, sir, I would just like to know what you call it." — "Well, Bill, my good fellow,

I can't tell you, for I know as little about religion as the mainmast; but I will tell the captain's wife's maid." In a few moments Bill was called into the cabin, and Alice said, "Bill, now tell me all about it." And Bill said, "You know, ma'am, that I did not go into the forecastle at all, but I just crept in under the topgallant forecastle, and there I just told Jesus what a big sinner I had been, and told him I wanted him to take away that load. For you know, ma'am, ever since that first meeting I could not sleep in my watch below; and I said, says I, 'What is the matter that I cannot sleep?' And then every thing I ever did in all my life came right up before me, ma'am; and I said, says I to myself, ma'am, you know, for I did not say any thing to my shipmates about it, 'What ails me?' And then, ma'am, don't you know my old mother, that I run away from fifteen years ago, seemed to say, 'Bill, you will be sorry for this.' And I tell you, ma'am, I was sorry. And right while I was praying, ma'am, there fell off from me a load of something like a man's falling from the maintop on deck. And I asked the second mate what he thought it was, if it was not religion; and he said he did not know any more about religion than the mainmast. And, ma'am, I feel better, now I have told you about it; and I think, ma'am, that your prayers have been answered, for I never felt so as I do now, ma'am, in all my life." And the great briny tears rolled down his weather-beaten face during the recital of what he had experienced. Alice told him she thought he could sleep now; and he went forward, singing as he went,—

"'Jesus loves me, and I love *him:*
That will *do,* that will *do.*
He set me free from all my *sin,*
And bid me go to work for *him:*
That will *do,* that will *do.*
In my whole life, never before,
Neither at sea, nor while on shore,
Have I loved him whom I adore:
That will do, *that will do.*"

His shipmates heard him singing; and they said, "What's the matter, Bill? Have you found a fortune?"— "Yes," says Bill, "I have got my pile now; and I mean to make this old forecastle ring with praise to Jesus."

Joe Windlass said, "You won't keep a fellow awake in his watch below; will you,.Bill?"

And Bill said, "Now, Joe, you know Bill Swan better. I sha'n't sing all the time; for I expect it will take a heap of praying to keep all my sails trimmed, and make the port of heaven in safety. But you know, Joe, that's where Bill is bound; and I intend to crowd all the canvas upon this old bark that she can carry, just as Capt. Shields crowds 'The Mary Alice' through the brine. And now, Joe, we have been shipmates on two voyages, and this is the third one; and you know Bill was always ready to divide the last cent with you, Joe. But this Jesus that I've got in here (striking his breast) I can't divide; but you can go to him, just as I did. And I tell you, Joe, that he will take your load away, just as he did mine; and I guess your load. is as big as mine, if not bigger, for you are an older man than I am. I think, when a fellow takes forty years to load up, that it takes him some little time to discharge that cargq; and I think, Joe, you had better begin to discharge, because, you know, if you should get a shot into that old hull of yours near the water-line, you might fill, founder, and sink before you got into port. You know, Joe, Capt. Shields told us last Sunday that no man was fit to die till he got a passport from Jesus; and I got that last night under the topgallant forecastle; and the captain's wife (God bless her!) and those other lady-passengers prayed for me till I told them to avast their praying, for my cargo of sin was discharged. But I tell you, Joe, it was not like hoisting up one barrel of sin at a time, as we hoist out cargo; but it was more like knocking out the whole bottom of the ship, and discharging the whole cargo at once, without stopping to rig a purchase."

Eight bells struck the hour of midnight. The pumps were tried, the watch called and relieved; and Bill and Joe, and the rest of the watch, went below for a four-hours sleep. At four A.M., when the watch was called, Bill said to Joe, "I have slept more this watch below than I have for three days and nights before." And Joe said,

"I believe I shall have to begin to discharge my cargo; for do you know, Bill, if I shut up my eyes, yet I could see just as plain as if they were open. I did not think a fellow could see with his eyes shut, before. You remember Bill, that night in New York, about two years ago, when we all had been taking a good swig at the landlord's bottle? Sam said he was the best sailor there; and I told him he could not show me any thing about a ship, from truck to keelson; and he called me a liar; and I knocked him over on to the stove, and gave him a big gash on his face. Now, Bill, he was right there all my watch below, and I saw him with his face all bloody; and I had my eyes shut all the time. Now, what do you make of that, Bill?"—"Well, Joe, it seems just as though, when the Lord wants us to discharge our cargo of sins, that he just makes us take a good look at them first, so that we may see how hateful we have been; and when we begin to hate them, and feel that we cannot remove them ourselves, and pray for him to do it, he comes and discharges the whole cargo in a moment: that is the way I found it. But look here, Joe, have you begun to pray yet?"—"No, Bill: I see no use of such a wicked man as I am praying."

"But avast there, Joe! if you fell overboard, you would sing out for some one to throw a rope's-end, I guess, for you to lay hold of. Now, that is what I call praying: it is just asking Jesus to do for us what we can't do for ourselves."

"Well, Bill, I understand now what praying means."

"Now, Joe, when the watch is out, if you like, I will go with you under the topgallant forecastle, and just ask Jesus to help you to unload. I shall never forget that place."

When the watch was changed, they sought the spot where Bill had found Jesus; and Joe began to tell Jesus what he had done. Bill cries, "Avast there, Joe! Jesus knows more about you than you can tell him; and all you have to do, Joe, is to ask him to take away your sins, and then believe he will do it, and he will unload you at once." Bill prayed in his simple but fervent spirit for his shipmate, that his sins might be forgiven. Then Joe

began to pray again, begging Jesus to have mercy upon
his guilty soul. In his prayer he said, "I know you
can save sinners, because you have saved Bill and Jack
Carter; and I am a bigger sinner than both of them
together; and Capt. Shields said last night that Jesus
came to seek and to save the lost. Lord, I am lost now.
Seek and save me, and I will serve thee all my life."

They then went below. At seven bells the watch was
called, and their breakfast sent them. While they were
eating breakfast, Joe said, "Bill, I feel something I never
felt before."

"What is it, Joe?"

"Well, somehow I feel kinder thankful for this breakfast, and I am sure I never felt so before." Eight bells
soon struck, and it was Joe's trick at the wheel. Perhaps an hour after, Capt. Shields came on deck, with
his wife clinging to his arm, for a promenade. After
walking back and forth a few minutes, he discovered that
something had happened to Joe, and wanted to ask him.
As he had forbidden any conversation with the man
at the wheel, and he would not violate his own order,
Capt. Shields said, "Joe, strike the relief bell." Immediately Sam came, and relieved him; and the captain
said, "Joe, my man, what is the matter with you?"

Well, you see, sir, I don't exactly know; but I know
one thing, that, while Bill and me was praying under the
topgallant forecastle, I got rid of a big load in about
one minute, and I have felt pretty well ever since. I
want to tell you, Capt. Shields, I have shipped and signed
papers for the whole voyage of life, and I will never quit
the ship till I get my discharge from Jesus my Saviour."

"Well, Joe, I have been expecting this, and I expect
to see all my men brought to Christ before our return to
B——."

That evening at four bells, when all were assembled,
they sung the hymn, "Rock of ages, cleft for me," &c.,
in which many of the men joined, and none sung sweeter
than Bill and Joe. After singing, Capt. Shields read a
portion of Scripture, where the duty of prayer was urged,
with its results. This, he said, had been fully proven
during the last twenty-four hours, in the conversion of two

of his men. After a few more remarks, he said, "We are about to bow in prayer: if any of my officers or men desire an especial remembrance in our petitions, I would like to have them speak out, without shame or fear."

The second officer, Mr. Boom, arose, and said he wished an interest in all their prayers. And Sam, who heard the conversation between Joe and the captain, said he wished he was as good as his captain : it was all he would ask. He would like for them to pray for him, if they thought they could make him a better man. Capt. Shields then told him that no person could make him better, but that Jesus could cleanse the vilest of sinners. He can save even to the uttermost, all that come unto God by him.

Bill said, " You all know Capt. Shields won't discharge this ship's cargo ; but he will get somebody to do it for him. When you are sick, — and I believe there are more sick ones here than Mr. Boom and Sam, — you send for the doctor to cure you, don't you? Well, now send for Jesus : he is the doctor, and he don't bring a long bill against you, either. He don't ask any pay. He cured me and Joe for nothing. Now, when you pray, that is just sending for him ; and now let us all pray." They all knelt in prayer, and Bill prayed first ; then Capt. Shields ; then Joe prayed ; then the captain's wife and her maid closed up that solemn season. Mr. Boom, the second officer, felt deeply his need of salvation through the night. He wanted to talk with Bill, who was in his watch ; but he was too proud to speak to one of the crew, fearing that insubordination might grow out of it, and so he refrained. About two days after, light broke in upon his mind, and he and Sam both seemed to be very happy.

Here had been four conversions, all in the starboard watch ; while there was but one Christian in the larboard watch, and that was Jack Carter. But such an increased number of praying souls were soon to shake both watches, till there would be but a few left to oppose the onward wave of religion through the ship.

A few days after, they spoke an English ship, from Madras for London, and requested to be reported. Every evening at six P.M., and every sabbath morn at ten A.M., that ship's company met for worship. Capt. Shields now ordered all three topgallant yards sent down, as they were drawing near the Cape. Here they experienced the first gale of wind, which was very heavy, from the south-west. While laying to, they caught several albatrosses, many of which measure, from one wing's end to the other, ten and twelve feet. They caught several Cape pigeons and Molly-mokes. After twelve hours the gale subsided, and they had a strong gale from the eastward, which they improved to the best advantage, pressing "The Mary Alice" with all the canvas she could bear. Two days after they passed Cape Horn, about ten miles distant, having been fifty-four days from B——.

In a few days after passing the Cape, the weather again began to assume a milder aspect, and topgallant and royal yards were sent aloft, and their additional canvas spread to the favoring breeze. Passed several vessels of different size and rig soon after they had passed the much-dreaded Cape Horn.

CHAPTER V.

SINCE our last report of the meetings on board, five more of the crew had shipped on board the good ship Zion, now making eight that had been led to Christ since they left B——. Alice had so kept up her singing-club, that they had a strong and very efficient choir. Singing upon the ocean is as much sweeter, and more subduing in its influence upon our hearts, as a good choir would surpass in sweetness the chatter of an ordinary parrot.

A very few days elapsed before they were again within the tropics, where another porpoise was caught, and several dolphins; and thousands of skipjacks were following . the ship from day to day. One of the men aloft espied a large shark in the ship's wake, following, to pick up whatever was thrown overboard by the cook. Mr. Helm, the first officer, said he would give Mr. Shark an invitation to come on board, if he would accept. He accordingly put a large piece of pork on the shark-hook; and, with a strong line bent to the hook, he threw it over the stern. It was quite moderate then, the ship going only about four miles per hour. Almost as soon as the hook had passed clear of the ship, the shark seized it in his voracious jaws; but when he found the hook was through his lower jaw, and he could not rid himself of the trouble, he thrashed, and made the water fly merrily for a while. But Mr. Shark was brought alongside, and a tackle upon the mainyard soon gave him a new element to try to live in; but he soon died after he was taken in upon deck. He measured nine feet and a half in length, and had six rows of teeth in each jaw. The passengers had heard much said about sharks, but never saw one before.

Two days after catching the shark, it had become so calm that the ship did not move; and a man who was aloft said there was something upon the surface of the

water, and he could not make out what it was. Capt.
Shields gave permission to Mr. Helm to lower one of the
boats, and go and see what it was. Mr. Helm took a
pair of grains and a harpoon with him, knowing there
would be a plenty of nice fish around it, to feed on the
clams that grow on any floating substance that has been
long in the ocean. They soon came to it; and Mr. Helm
had some rare sport, and did not stop till he had caught
twenty or more very fine fish with his grains, which he
would dart into the fish, and instantly pull him on board.

They made a rope fast to the cask, for such it proved
to be, and towed it alongside the ship. A tackle was in
readiness as soon as they came. They slung the cask
with ropes, and soon hoisted it on board, and the boat
was hoisted up and secured. Men were set at work to
scrape off the clams from the cask; and it was thought it
would hold one hundred and twenty gallons, and perhaps
more. After finding the bung, it was soon knocked out,
and the cask was found to contain the most beautiful cordial that any person on board had ever seen. The captain ordered the cask bunged again, and put into the
ship's storeroom.

A few hours after, they took the south-east trades, that
bore them rapidly on their way. The meetings, in the
mean while, had never flagged. Almost every evening
some unusual anxiety would be manifested by some who
had never shown any interest before. Five more of the
crew and the third officer were made to rejoice in the Lord
by the effectual working-power of the Holy Spirit, making,
in all, fourteen that had forsaken the ways of sin, and had
been made to rejoice in Jesus their Saviour since their
sailing from B——.

A very painful accident or providence occurred one
day. Bill was at work in the maintop, and by some
means fell. He caught hold of one of the main bunt-
lines while coming down; but his hold was broken, and
he fell upon deck. He had a cut in his forehead, and
had broken his left arm, and received some other bruises.
Alice said, "Dear husband, we have plenty of spare rooms
in the house; and I want Bill brought in here, so that I
can take care of him."

"It shall be as you wish, my darling. Oh, what should I do and what should I be, if I had a proud, selfish, and unfeeling wife! Alice dear, do you not know I could not live with such a woman twenty-four hours?" After Bill was brought into the house, Capt. Shields said, "How I wish I was a good surgeon, that I might put this broken arm together as it ought to be!"

Dr. A—— then said to Capt. Shields, "I am a regularly trained surgeon and physician of the old school, but thought I would not make known my official business unless there was an opportunity for me to use my skill and experience."

Capt. Shields said in reply, "I shall be very glad to turn my dear shipmate over to you, Dr. A——, with this proviso, that I be allowed to learn all I can; so that, if an occasion should ever occur in my future experience, I might be benefited myself, and be the better able to benefit some fellow-sufferer."

Dr. A—— said, "My dear captain, it will not only be a pleasure to have your presence, but I may need your assistance; and I can give you some practical lessons in surgery if you desire them." Dr. A—— and Capt. Shields went into Bill's room, where the poor fellow lay groaning; and Dr. A—— very soon set the broken arm, sewed up the wound on his face, and applied some liniment to his other wounds and bruises. He then gave him a mild opiate, and said he hoped he would sleep quietly for some hours, that his naturally strong physical structure might gather strength by quiet rest to grapple with the shock it had received.

Capt. Shields said, "Dr. A——, I feel extremely thankful for what I have been permitted to see and hear, and shall treasure it up, as we sailors say, in my locker, to be called out, if ever needed."

Bill, under Dr. A——'s judicious treatment and Alice's gentle nursing, began to recover rapidly. When he first awoke from his eight-hours' sleep, and opened his eyes, he seemed somewhat astonished. Alice saw he was confused, and said to him, "Bill, you must lie perfectly quiet; for you have had a terrible fall, — broke your arm, cut your face, and bruised yourself all over, — and I had you brought into this room, that I might take care of you till you get well; and I want you to do just as Dr. A—— and I tell you, and all will be well."

"My God!" said Bill, "what have I done, to be used in this way? I am nothing but an old, broken-down hulk, anyhow; and, if that buntline had only been fast on deck, I would not have been here now. But, ma'am, I have no business here, anyway. And then to think of having my dear captain's wife to care for my old, half-wrecked hull is more than I can bear, ma'am." And Bill burst out a-crying like a grieved child.

Alice said, "Bill, we must be Christians something more than in name only. Remember, Jesus says, 'All things, therefore, that ye would that others should do to you, do ye even so to them;' and I know, Bill, if you saw me in danger, you would come to my relief."

"Why, God bless you, ma'am! If I should see you fall overboard, I would leap into the sea in a moment to save you, even if got drowned: but, ma'am, there is no danger of that, for I can swim like a fish. I was once three days on a broken mainyard in the sea, and two of my ship-mates with me, ma'am; and they was both drowned, and I was the only one that was saved. But you won't fall overboard. God always will take care of his angels, and I am sure you are one of them, ma'am."

Alice, smiling at Bill's story, said, "You must not think or call me an angel, for I am not; and the Bible teaches us that all the angels that have ever been seen upon earth were men. There is no account in the Bible of such a being as a female angel."

"But," says Bill, "I know I have seen many pictures of angels, and I never see any that was not women."

"That is all true, Bill. But those pictures have been gotten up to create sympathy; and, by appealing to people's sympathy, they hope to make money by their pictures."

"I see," said Bill: "it is something like my painting (if I could) a cotton-factory, with all the cog-wheel fixings, which I had never seen."

Alice laughed heartily at Bill's funny comparison, and said, "Yes, Bill, it would be something like it."

When Alice met her husband in their room alone, she said, "Johnny, that man Bill is a gem under a very rough exterior."

Capt. Shields said, "He is only a perfect type of the great mass of our seamen."

Alice replied, saying, "I know it is true of my dear Johnny, and I believe it is true of Bill; for he said, if I should fall overboard, he would jump after me in a moment."

"Yes," says her husband; "and there are not two sailors on board this ship to-day, but would do the same thing if they thought there was any possibility, or even probability, of saving your life, my dear Alice. You have many things to learn yet of the intrinsic excellences of a thorough sailor's character."

"She replied, saying, "I am in school now, my dear Johnny, and shall avail myself of all my surroundings from day to day to become fitted more perfectly to be a practical sailor's wife. But, Johnny dear, there is one thing that I wish very much to learn; and that is the theory of navigation, so that, if any thing should happen to you, I might be able to navigate the ship myself."

"Just like your own self, my ever-precious Alice. You shall receive your first lesson to-day."

"Well, Johnny dear, when you get ready for me, please send Annie for me. I must go now, and relieve Annie for a while, and look after my patient." As soon as she made her appearance in Bill's room, he began to weep; and she asked him why he wept. "Well, you see, ma'am, I have not got a single shot in my old locker. I have always spent it for whiskey; and all my wages won't half pay you for what you have done to keep this old hull of mine from foundering, and going to the bottom to make grub for sharks. Anyhow, ma'am, you shall have all my wages; and I don't see as how I can do any better, if I give you all I've got. Well, you see, I can't do any more. That's fair now, ain't it, ma'am?"

By the time Bill had got through with expressing his intentions, Alice was in tears; and Bill, not apprehending the cause, said, "Ma'am, don't cry; for, if I can't pay the whole amount, it may be Jesus will give you the balance from his locker, for he has been pretty busy in handing out the best coin I ever saw. There is Joe and Sam and Harvey and Jack and the second mate, and old Bill; and I tell you, ma'am, I am just as happy here as I can be."

Alice told him she got her pay from Jesus every day, and he would never have a cent to pay. "Now, Bill, I hope you will never think of this again. But I want to ask you one question, Bill; and that is, when we arrive at San Francisco, and you go on shore with your shipmates, whether you will drink any more whiskey, as you have done in your past life."

"Why, God bless you, ma'am! didn't I tell Jesus, if he would just forgive me, and discharge the wicked cargo I had been taking in every day of my life, that I never would take any more such cargo into this old hull of mine? And don't ye know, ma'am, he discharged my whole cargo in a minute, and he didn't stop to rig a tackle; and now, ma'am, do you think I will ever go back on Jesus, who has done all this for me? I tell you, ma'am, Bill don't ever treat his shipmates in that kind of a way; and I am sure I love Jesus too well to do that thing. And, if the land-sharks bait their hooks for a bite, I know of one fish they will never catch; and that's old Bill. Why, God bless ye, ma'am! I know all them old land-sharks. Have they not caught me by the gills in Boston, New York, Charleston, New Orleans, and in London and Liverpool and Calcutta, and I don't know how many other places, for I have forgot some of them? I want to tell you, ma'am, they have caught old Bill for the last time. Why, ma'am, I don't never forget what I remember, and I don't suppose anybody does; but the captain read at the last meeting I went to before I was thrown on my beam-ends, that they that trust in the Lord shall be as Mount Zion, that cannot be removed, but abideth forever. Thinks I to myself, thinks I, 'That means you, Bill.' Now, if I trust in Jesus, I cannot be removed. It's a kind of bargain, ain't it, ma'am? If I trust, he will keep me. Ain't it so, ma'am? That is the way it seems to me. Now, ma'am, am I right, or wrong? You know all about it; and I want you should tell me, for I want to be just right, and, if I am wrong, I want to know that, so as to do better."

Alice then told Bill she thought he was all right, and that he was tired, and needed rest, and thought he had better not talk any more till some other time ; and he, like an obedient child, soon fell asleep.

During all this time "The Mary Alice" was making rapid strides towards her destined port. Two more of the men, and Mr. Helm the first officer, had found Jesus precious to their souls as their Saviour. Bill had not yet returned to duty, but was well enough to mingle with his shipmates in the forecastle. Alice had become so well versed in the theory of navigation, that she could make up the ship's day's work, as we sailors term it, quicker than her husband, and fully as accurate. That day they spoke the ship "Hector," from San Francisco, bound to the Sandwich Islands, only four days out, and requested her to report.

All hands were now busy in scouring and cleaning ship, so as to make as good an impression as it was possible to make. At ten A.M., two days after speaking "The Hector," land was discovered ahead ; and "The Mary Alice," crowded by a press of canvas, soon came in near the land, and set signal for a pilot, the ship laying with her maintopsail aback, waiting. Very soon one was discovered standing towards the ship, and very soon the pilot was on board, and sail made ; and in threee hours after, "The Mary Alice" was anchored abreast of the city, sails all neatly furled, yards all squared by lifts and braces. Capt. Shields then asked the pilot if the ship "C," from New York, had arrived, and was told she had not. He then remarked, "She ought to be here, for she sailed ten days before me. He hoped nothing had happened to her. Capt. Shields went on shore, reported the arrival of the ship "Mary Alice," one hundred and two days from B——, commanded by John Shields. He then went to the custom-house, and, after finishing his business there, returned to his ship. He ordered Mr. Helm to call all hands aft. Capt. Shields said to them, "You have all done your duties faithfully, and to my satisfaction, and to the satisfaction of my officers. And now, as many of you as wish to remain by the ship, to go with me again, please to place yourselves on the starbord side of the deck:" all but two went over. He then said to the two men, "You are now discharged from further duty; but, if you wish to remain by the ship for a week, I shall not charge you for your board. I will pay you off to-morrow. You can now go forward."

Dr. A—— asked Capt. Shields if he knew where he should go from there. He told him that at present he did not know; but his ship was new, and would command the highest freights, and he should be on the alert to accept the first profitable offer made him.

The next day "The Mary Alice" was hauled in to the wharf. No sooner was she made fast than the sailor-land-lords, in numbers, rushed on board, expecting a rich har-vest from so large a ship as "The Mary Alice." Bill went aft, and asked permission of Capt. Shields to give those sailor-landlords a bit of a talk. The captain seemed to wait; but Alice said, "Give him permission. I want to hear him."

Capt. Shields said, "Bill, I have no objection, if you don't insult them: that will not benefit either you or them."

Bill went forward; and one of them said, "Are you a-going to remain by the ship? You can get twenty dol-lars per month to go anywhere to almost any port." Bill then mounted the topgallant forecastle, and said, so every one on board and many on shore could hear, "Now, shipmates and sailor-landlords, I have found a floating heaven on board this good ship 'Mary Alice;' and I don't propose to leave her, unless my dear captain turns me adrift." And all the crew cried out, "Amen! you have spoken our minds." And Joe exclaimed, "The most of us have learned to let well enough alone."

One landlord after another left the ship; and, as they were going over the ship's side, Bill struck up the hymn he had sung, as if by inspiration, when he was converted: —

"Jesus loves me, and I love him:
That will do, that will do.
He set me free from all my sin,
And bids me go to work for him:
That will do, that will do.

In my whole life, never before,
Neither at sea, nor while on shore,
Have I loved him I now adore:
That will do, that will do."

The landlords left, cursing all the psalm-singing sailors on board, and all other Christians generally. After Capt. Shields and his wife had entered the cabin, Alice said, "I told you dear old Bill would do the thing just right."

"But, Alice dear, I cannot conceive where that old tar got his poetical ingenuity from ; for that was a splendid composition. I have never heard any thing about it before."

Alice said she had never heard it sung before. But Mr. Boom said, "He sung it the night he was converted, and told me about it at that time. I believe he must have been inspired by the Spirit of God at that moment ; for I can see that his education has been very limited indeed." Her husband said he did not believe he ever went to school a day in his life.

Mr. Shields and his wife went on shore as soon as the ship was hauled in to the wharf. Dr. A—— called Capt. Shields into his room ; and, when they were alone, he said, "I am on a voyage of pleasure, and relaxation from my professional duties ; and, with your consent, I propose to make your ship my home or headquarters till I find where you go when you leave this place."

Capt. Shields replied by saying it would be very pleasing to him, as well as to his wife. He then added, "I suppose you know the peculiar condition of my wife. That has made me hesitate somewhat in accepting a freight which has been offered me to-day, and I only have two more days to accept or reject that freight. They offer me a very fair freight to Australia, with a cargo of wheat."

Dr. A—— said, if he should conclude to accept their proposition, he should wish to remain and go with him.

Capt. Shields then said to Dr. A——, —

"If I accept that freight, will you go as a passenger with me?" Dr. A—— gave him an affirmative reply.

"I will see what Alice says about the arrangement, and let you know." Alice was perfectly delighted ; for she had become very warmly attached to Dr. A—— ever since she saw his skill and judicious treatment with Bill. That matter permanently settled, Alice was more cheerful than she had been for several days.

By the 1st of March they began to take in their cargo for Australia; and on the 20th of March they sailed, but not till Capt. Shields had discharged his carpenter, and promoted Bill to the office of carpenter and boatswain. Bill was overwhelmed with gratitude to his captain for his promotion, and said he would try to do his duty. "The Mary Alice" sailed with a fair wind, and with grateful hearts to God for all his blessings upon them; and in their first evening meeting it was evident to all that God's Spirit was with them of a truth. One after another of the men spoke of Jesus' love to them. Joe said he was ashore one day, and a man asked him to go into a saloon. He went in, and the man went to the counter, and called for a drink; and he took it, and then handed it to Joe, saying, "Now drink that to my good health." Joe replied, "I am done drinking poison to other people's good health for the sake of destroying my own." Capt. Shields said, "You gave him a reply which I hope he will ever remember. Ever remember, my men, that, if you resist temptations, Jesus will help you. His word says he will not suffer us to be tempted above that we are able to bear, but with the temptation will provide a way of escape, that we may be able to bear it. Now, I wish, that, during our long passage, every man will study his Bible every day, so that you may become strong Christians, and intelligent, active, working Christians. You all know how long it took you to become what we call an able seaman, so as to know what to do with a ship at all times and under all circumstances. Now, on this passage, I have to get the sun at noon, and make up my day's work, and then mark our place on the chart every day, so that I may know where I am. Just so every Christian man and woman ought to study the Bible, for it is both chart and compass to the Christian; and by daily study you can find out where you are, and what your prospects are for reaching the port of heaven in safety."

Time rolled on, and the good ship was making her way rapidly on her passage. The sabbath services and daily prayer-meetings were always full of interest, and the singing never flagged. Bill's hymn was sung by all as their favorite. But Bill, having received a handle to his name by his promotion, must be called Bill no longer, but Mr. Mainstay; and by that name he will be known and called in the future.

CHAPTER VI

ON the first day of April, Alice made a present to her husband of a beautiful daughter, with which he seemed delighted, particularly when Dr. A—— assured him that his wife was very comfortable, and doing nicely. Annie was with her mistress, whom she loved as tenderly as her own sister. When the babe was about two weeks old, Mrs. Shields one day said, "I think you told me that you came from Vermont. Annie said she did, and said, "That makes me think of something. May I leave you long enough to go to my trunk? I will be back in a moment." Mrs. Shields said, "Certainly."

In a few moments she returned with a sealed package with this inscription on the envelope : "This package not to be opened till after my death. Signed, *Annie Baker, Vermont, January,* 1852." Now, my dear mistress, whatever this package may contain, it will certainly be right to open it now." Annie tore open the envelope, and in it was a most beautiful picture. As soon as Alice saw it, she at once exclaimed, "O me!" Annie asked her what she saw in it that so surprised her ; and Alice said, "It is the image of my only dear sister Mary, only I see now that it looks older than she is. Now, Annie dear, read me the contents of that package, if you have no objections to my knowing its secrets." Annie said, "I desire to have no secrets from you, my dear mistress."

"'This paper, my dear child, will give you a perfect knowledge of your right name, and the names of both of your parents, now in heaven I have no doubt. Your father's name was Alfred Bird. He was a cárpenter by trade, and married Miss Annie Bliss, the only sister of Mary Bliss, who was married to some person in G——, but I have forgotten his name.'" Mrs. Shields then said to Annie, "Call Capt. Shields in." She immediately called him ; and, when he came in, Alice asked him his mother's maiden name, and he told her it was Mary Bliss. "My dear Johnny, permit me to introduce to you your own cousin, Annie Bird. Why, Johnny dear, how good the blessed Jesus is to us poor sinners ! " — " Well, my dear Alice, that makes me think of that beautiful hymn of Watts's, ' God moves in a mysterious way, his wonders to perform,' " &c. "Well, now read on, my own sweet cousin Annie," said the happy Alice. " ' In about a year after their marriage, they moved into my neighborhood, and Mr. Bird bought a little farm ; but in six months after Mr. Bird died very suddenly with a lung-fever. Three months after, a daughter was born ; and the mother said, " If I should not live, name this child Annie Bliss Bird." I was called to nurse Mrs. Bird. She only lived about twelve hours after her child was born ; and the selectmen said they would put the child in the almshouse, and sell the farm for her support. I told them they never should send that child to the almshouse. Although I was a poor widow, I would share the last crumb with that child. I then said to the selectmen, "I wish you would sell the farm, and put the proceeds in the savings bank at B—— in the name of Annie B. Bird." In a month after, the farm was sold for the sum of five hundred dollars ; and not a cent of principal or interest has ever been drawn, as you will see by the date of your bank-book, which I enclose in this package. I did not think best in my lifetime to break up the motherly feelings which I have ever entertained towards you. You well remember, that, when you were fifteen years of age, you said, "Mother, I am old enough to get my own living, and not be such a tax upon you." And I finally consented, and you went to Boston, and went as an apprentice to learn a vest-maker's trade. The next year I found my health was failing me. I made my will, and have put it in trust for you, into the hands of Rev. Mr. B——, whom you well know.' "

Annie lifted up her hands with astonishment, saying, "I never heard of my mother's death." Alice said, "But she was not your mother." — "I know it now. But she was all the mother I ever knew ; and I loved her then, and ever shall love her,— more now, a thousand times more, than I ever did before. Oh, how few poor widows would have made the sacrifice she made to keep me out of the almshouse, and then to educate me besides! for my mother was a well-educated woman. I have been to school but very little; but my mother gave me lessons every day, and it always seemed so easy to learn from her! she always made every thing so plain and easy for me! My mother's name was Annie Baker. The word Bliss I never remember hearing my mother mention; and the letter B was unknown to me in connection with my name. I have never known any other name but Annie Baker. But oh, my dear, patient, suffering mother! And I knew nothing about it."

Alice then asked Annie how long it had been since she had received a letter from her; and Annie said she could not tell till she went to her trunk, and found her last letter. She went, and soon returned with a letter, with a postmark on the envelope "Brattleborough, May, 1853." "My mother put this package into the bottom of my trunk, and I never saw it till about two months ago."

"That is but a little more than a year before I was married," said Alice. "We were married in June, 1854. But I am anxious to hear that letter, my dear cousin Annie Bliss Bird. What a beautiful name! And you have ever been a blissful bird to me, dear Annie; and now, when we find such good authority proving that you are my own dear cousin, I think it blissful indeed. But let us have that letter now: I can wait no longer."

DUMMERSTON, May, 1853.

My dear daughter, I have waited for some time, hoping to hear from you; but, as I have not heard from you for more than a month, I thought I would write, and let you know how anxious I am to hear from you. I send this by Mr. B———, to be mailed at Brattleborough to you; and I wish you to let me hear from you on receipt of this. I am enjoying as good health as usual; but I have nothing of importance to write more, more than that my dear Annie may ever remember my counsel to go out but little evenings in that wicked city, where so many alluring nets are set to entrap the young and unsuspecting; for, in giving you such advice, I only have your future good at heart. Reply as soon as you receive this. From your ever dear mother to her beloved daughter Annie.

ANNIE BAKER.

"Well, my dear Annie," said Alice, "I do not wonder

that you love such a mother; for that is a letter of excellent counsel, Annie dear. And now one more question: When did you reply to this excellent letter?"

"I can soon tell you, cousin Alice," said Annie; "for, ever since my dear mother instructed me, I have kept a receipt-book, in which I have entered every letter received, and all I have written, and I have often found it convenient for reference."

Alice replied, saying she thought her mother must be a very methodical woman; and Annie said she ought to be, for she was a Methodist in every sense of that word.

Annie brought her receipt-book, and found that she had replied to that letter June 30, 1853. Alice then asked if that was the last letter she had received or written; and Annie said that was the last entry on her receipt-book. "Stop a moment. I really believe I remember of another letter." And she went and found it in her dress-pocket. It was dated in D——, April, 1854, and contained similar advice to the other.

Annie said, "I know I must have answered it, although, for some reason, I failed to record either of them; and I am certain this was my mother's last letter."

Alice then said, "Your dear mother may be living to-day, for aught you know, dear Annie."

"That is true," said Annie; "and I have broken open this package without knowing whether she was dead or alive." And Annie wept like a child, saying, "I would do nothing to displease my precious dear mother. Alice endeavored to comfort her, saying it was a sin of ignorance, if it could be called a sin.

Annie said, "That is what pains me: I had no right to open the package till I knew my mother was dead."

"Well, Annie dear, the deed is done; and I know by those tears, that you are heartily sorry; and I know Jesus will forgive you; and I think your dear mother would also forgive you, if she knew all the circumstances: so cheer up, my dear cousin, and let us believe all will be well."

We must leave the two cousins for the present, to see how Capt. Shields quelled a plot which was intended to result in a mutiny. Our readers will remember that

Capt. Shields discharged two men in San Francisco, and shipped two men to fill their places. The name of one was Bob, and the other Fred. After sailing, neither of these two men ever attended the evening prayer-meeting. This was noticed by Capt. Shields and by all the men; and they very reluctantly attended the sabbath-morning services. The first and third mates were both in the larboard watch together, Mr. Helm, the first mate, having sole charge of the deck. And here I wish to remark that Mr. Helm was a splendid seaman and navigator, and was very highly esteemed by Capt. Shields and by all the crew except Bob and Fred.

After being at sea a few days, Mr. Helm noticed that the third officer, Mr. Head, was forward with the men the most of his watch upon deck in the night. He thought it best to say nothing to him, but strictly and quietly watch results. One very calm though dark night, he noticed that Mr. Head went forward very soon after he came upon deck; and Mr. Helm felt, for some reason he could not explain, a degree of uneasiness which he never felt before. These two men, Fred and Bob, were both in his watch, and he went forward to see that every thing was right. Jack Carter came to him, and said in a low voice, "Bob and Fred are trying to kick up a row, and I thought it best to let you know it, sir; and I think Mr. Head is in for a share somewhere."

"Thank you, Jack! Keep dark, and watch them, and, if you learn any thing more, report to me at once." — "Ay, ay, sir!" said Jack. Mr. Helm went aft again; but he was restless. In a few minutes after he went forward again, and overheard Mr. Head say, "I will provide you with pistols from the arm-chest, and lock it, so that they can get no weapons to help themselves with, and we will have them in a tight fix." Bob said, "We can fasten them all below, and then we can just put one of them in soak at a time, that will not submit to our articles of faith and practice." Fred said, "We shall find both hands full when we come to deal with Jack Carter and old Joe, who are both in our watch: they are as strong as a couple of horses, and they don't fear the devil, neither of them."

Mr. Helm quietly retired. He then very pleasantly called Mr. Head aft, saying, "Take charge of the deck for a few minutes, sir;" and he went into the house, and made Capt. Shields acquainted with the whole programme. Capt. Shields then said, "Without the rest of the watch knowing it, send me Joe and Jack Carter." It was done in a few moments. He then said, "Send that man Bob to me at once." Mr. Helm said, "He may be armed." — "Send him at once, sir! He will soon find he has no coward to deal with."

Mr. Helm called Bob to him, and said, "The captain wants to see you in the cabin." Bob thought he was going to give him a talk, because he had not attended meetings : so into the cabin he went, without the least suspicion of the reception he would receive. As soon as he entered, Joe closed the door, and stood against it. Capt. Shields then said, "Bob, I have a pair of handcuffs here that will fit you, I think. Reach out your hands, and try them on." Bob said, "What does this mean?" Capt. Shields, in a voice like thunder, said, "I do not parley with mutineers! — Jack, put on these irons!" Jack said, "Now, Bob, if you want to keep the breath in you, it will be better for you to submit at once." Bob, looking the situation in the face, held out his hands, and Jack put his wrist-ruffles on at once.

Capt. Shields then ordered him to sit down. He then said to Joe, "Go upon deck, and tell Mr. Helm to send Fred into the cabin." In a few moments he came ; and, when he saw Bob there already in irons, he knew it was all up with him, and he submitted to be put in irons without saying a word. The captain then sent for Mr. Head ; and when he came in, and saw the two men with whom he had planned a wholesale drowning or butchery, he was overwhelmed with astonishment, and wished to make some explanation. But Capt. Shields, in a voice of thunder, exclaimed, "Silence, sir! not a word from you, sir! — Jack Carter, go upon deck, and take charge of the deck, and send Mr. Helm to me, sir." Mr. Helm was in the cabin in a few moments ; and Capt. Shields said to him, "Have these three men put between decks, with Joe to watch them, until eight bells in the morning."

Now, this whole matter was so quietly conducted, that none except the watch upon deck knew any thing about it. At eight bells in the morning, Capt. Shields ordered Mr. Helm to call all hands aft; and this strange, unusual call brought Dr. A—— and wife, and Alice and Annie, out upon the quarter-deck. After all his men had come aft, he then said, "Mr. Helm, you will please bring the prisoners upon deck." When they saw Mr. Head, Bob, and Fred led on deck by Joe, in irons, they were all astonished. Capt. Shields then said, "These three men had already plotted a mutiny, in which any persons on board not submitting to their authority and dictation, were, to use their own language, to be put in soak, or, in other words, were to be thrown overboard and drowned. Providentially the plot was discovered before they had time to execute their hellish design. Neither of these men, under any circumstances, will be returned to duty again. I now promote Jack Carter as my third officer; and I know my men well enough to believe that every man on board of this ship will obey his orders as the third officer of this ship in the future. — Mr. Carter, you will please accept the office, and I will pay you the same wages as I paid the mutinous villain who once filled that office."

The prisoners were then ordered between decks, with Joe for their watchman. The captain then told Mr. Helm he had better take Dick and Sam out of the starboard watch, to better equalize the strength of the men in the two watches. Capt. Shields then said, "Men, you have all ever been well treated by myself and my officers, and ever will be, so long as you continue to be respectful and obedient to my officers, and do your duty. But insubordination or disobedience cannot exist one moment on board of this ship; and any man who attempts it will find in me a hard master. You may now go to your duties."

At the dinner-table Capt. Shields told Dr. A—— and his wife how the plot was discovered, and what Mr. Helm had heard. Dr. A—— remarked that he never liked Mr. Head: he saw things on their passage to San Francisco that led him to dislike the man. "One night, while Mr. Mainstay was sick, I went out upon deck, and heard him

tell some of the men he did not believe, if he had fell
from aloft, instead of that psalm-singing Bill, that the
captain's wife would have nursed him as she had done
him (old Bill, as he called him)." Alice replied by saying that she would have done the same thing for any man
on board: she somehow looked upon them as all being
members of their ship's family; and in that respect she
had no partiality for one more than another. "That is
spoken just like yourself, my dear Alice," said Capt.
Shields. Turning to Dr. A——, he said, "Our sweet
little daughter has not been named yet, though she is
more than two months old." Dr. A—— said, "If she
were my daughter, I should have called her Mary Alice as
soon as she was born, in honor of this noble floating pal-
ace where she first came into existence." Alice said she
did not see how she could have any other name, without
casting some reflections upon her aunt, mother, and their
beautiful floating home. Capt. Shields said that name
was the sweetest name to him in the world; and he wanted
it perpetuated.

During their passage thus far, Dick and Jim had both
found their Saviour, and were rejoicing in his forgiving
love. All hands were now busy in painting their ship
inside, for they were drawing near to their intended port.
A few days after, land was discovered; and that morning
they had caught another porpoise, for which they were
very thankful; for every thing fresh in the shape of pigs
and chickens had been gone for more than a week, and
the porpoise came very acceptable indeed. In the afternoon they took a pilot, and about sunset they anchored
in the harbor of Melbourne, after a passage of eighty-four
days from San Francisco. Arriving June 12, 1855, the
next day the prisoners were carried on shore, to be sent
to B—— for their trial, with all the testimony of their
guilt, taken under oath, to be sent with them. In little
more than a week the ship was discharged, and began to
take in a freight for London.

While they were there, an epidemic broke out; and
Capt. Shields forbade his men going on shore, fearing it
might be brought on board his ship; and Dr. A—— sec-
onded this judicious caution. He talked with his men,

and told them that he was obliged to be on shore to attend to the business of his ship; and Sam said there was not a man on board "The Mary Alice" that would do any thing to displease their dear captain. Capt. Shields shipped three new men in the places of the mutineers. A few days before sailing, a gentleman came on board, and asked if he could take passage with him, with his wife and his brother. Capt. Shields informed him that he could accommodate them; and they soon came on board, and were introduced to Dr. A—— and wife, and to his own wife and cousin, and to his officers. They sailed July 6, only remaining there twenty-four days. Capt. Shields said his despatch was wholly owing to the epidemic, which he feared might be contagious. The new passengers were surprised to hear the captain ask God to bless their food before they ate. At four bells they were still more surprised to see the whole crew, and the three new men with them, come aft to attend their daily meeting. It was a new and a novel sight to them; but, when they heard these old tars of Neptune sing and pray as they did that night, they were awestruck and attentive. On Sunday they had a very interesting service; for Mr. Albert Shields, the elder brother of the two new passengers, said, "I believe God has sent this ship to Melbourne to save my soul. I experienced religion in Limerick, where I was born, more than thirty years ago; and I well remember my uncle John's advice. He said, 'Albert, don't leave your father. I have no father to leave, and shall go to America.' But in a few years afterwards I left my home, and came to Melbourne; and I have made an earthly fortune; but oh, how dark and drear are my prospects for heaven, which once were so bright and promising! I hope every praying soul on board this ship will daily pray that God may forgive my sins, and let his love again shine in upon my benighted soul."

The younger brother said he had only been a little more than a year with his brother, and that he was enjoying much of Jesus' love, and was much pleased that he was going home in a praying ship. After the meeting was dismissed, the ever-inquisitive Alice said to Mr. Albert

Shields, "I think you said, sir, that your uncle, who came to America, was named John Shields?" He replied, saying, "Yes. And my father said he guessed John would do well; for he had learned a blacksmith's trade, and had plenty of work."

"Annie dear, please call my husband." When he came in, she said, "My dear Johnny, permit me to introduce to you two more of your own cousins; and the two men clasped hands; and the captain said, "Alice dear, what does this all mean?" And Alice said, "Your dear father came from Limerick to B——, and went and learned a blacksmith's trade, and so wrote to his brother there, informing him of the fact. One question I wish to ask, which will settle the whole matter at once. What was your grandmother Shields's given name?" He replied, "It was Eunice."—"Then we are cousins, sure enough. I have often heard my father say his mother was Aunt Eunice to almost everybody."—"Well, Alice dear, do you think you will be fortunate enough to find any more new cousins for your husband?"—"Well, Johnny, I can tell you better after we leave London, and see if you will be kind enough to furnish me with the necessary material. You know I cannot make brick without straw."

CHAPTER VII.

WHILE the new cousin-making was progressing, "The Mary Alice" was progressing with rapidity towards the Cape of Good Hope; and Alice perceived that young Ernest Shields and Annie had become very intimate with each other, and playfully remarked to Annie one day, that she thought ere long she would become a double cousin to her. Annie blushed, saying, "Dear Alice, you had better wait till you see the marriage-ceremony performed before you count on that relationship." Alice merely remarked, "We shall see: time ultimately discloses events."

Mary Alice, jun., had become the plaything of all on board. When the child was on deck in pleasant weather, every tar in the ship would catch the dear child up in his arms, and give her a kiss, just as though she belonged to all hands on board. Mr. Carter seemed to be the child's favorite. He would sometimes enclose her in his brawny arms, and carry her for an hour at a time when he was idle. But an event occurred some fifteen days after they sailed, that filled every soul on board that ship with painful anxiety. Capt. Shields was suddenly severely seized with a high fever and with terrible cramp-spasms. Dr. A—— was soon at his side, and told his wife not to fear. He thought, if he could throw all care and responsibility aside, he could soon relieve him. Alice said, "Now, Johnny dear, I will keep your reckoning up every day, and report our position to you every day; and you know, Johnny, that you can trust your Alice to navigate the ship without infringing upon any of the rights of Mr. Helm, your first officer."

At evening Mr. Helm conducted the meeting; and it was a prayer-meeting indeed, and such a one as never was known before on board "The Mary Alice." Never

before did Alice realize the deep, tender, and ardent
affection those men all had for her dear husband.   She
told her husband, some time after that, she should love
sailors as long as she lived.   "Why, after Sam, and Joe,
and Dick, and Mr. Boom, and Mr. Carter, and Mr. Mainstay, and our dear Mr. Helm, had prayed, I felt that I
understood that passage of Scripture which says, 'The
kingdom of heaven suffereth violence, and the violent
take it by force.'   Why, Johnny, I never heard or saw
such pleading importunity in my life.   It was like good
old Jacob wrestling with the angel, with an unshaking
confidence that could not be turned away; and somehow
that passage of Scripture came into my mind, 'All things
are possible to him that believeth; only believe and he
shall live.'   And, Johnny dear, from that praying-hour I
felt sure of your restoration to health."

It was true he rapidly began to amend.   They had
just got soundings on the bank of the Cape, and the next
day they had safely passed it, and were pressing their
way towards St. Helen's, or what is called St. Helena,
where they arrived after a passage of fifty-two days
from Melbourne.   They arrived Aug. 26, 1855.   In eight
hours they made all sail for home.   Capt. Shields had so
far recovered as to take the charge of their meetings
again.   The three men that came on board at Melbourne, in seeing the answers of prayer in regard to
their captain, were deeply impressed; and in a few days,
through the instruction of Joe, Sam, and Dick, they were
led to trust in Jesus, and to rejoice in his pardoning love.

It very soon became evident to all in the cabin that
Mr. Ernest Shields was earnestly pressing his suit with
Miss Annie Bird; and Alice said one day, "I expect,
when we arrive in London, that my now blissful Bird
will take wings, and fly into a bosom of Shields for protection." — "Well, my dear cousin Alice, do you not
think I should find ample protection in such a Shield?"

"Well, Annie dear, I have unbounded confidence in my
Shields; and, if your Shields is as good as mine, I think
he is rightly called Ernest." — "Now, cousin Alice, be
sober; for I want your advice.   Mr. Shields has made
proposals to me; and I did not feel at liberty to give

him a final reply until I had first laid the whole matter before you and your husband." — "Johnny is at liberty now: please tell him I wish to see him in my room." She went and called him, and in a few minutes they were closeted alone.

Alice told him of Ernest's proposal. He then said he had been having a conversation with Albert relative to this same matter, and he made a very rigid inquiry in regard to her character, accomplishments, &c.; and, after giving his consent to me, he said he would see his brother, and consent to their union, adding, "I have promised to give him ten thousand dollars to begin the world with if he married a woman that I could approve of." — "Well, then," said Alice, "as soon as we get in London I will draw upon my father, and give her a splendid outfit."

They were now approaching their destined haven very rapidly, daily passing ships and steamers; and they exchanged signals with one of our steam packet-ships bound to London, and gave the name of their ship. As the wind was ahead, the steamer was soon out of sight. The next morning they took a pilot, and he very soon brought the ship to anchor at Gravesend. They had not anchored more than an hour, before a steam-tug was seen approaching them. She soon hailed the ship, and asked if they wanted steam. Capt. Shields said, "Yes: come alongside." She was no sooner securely fastened to "The Mary Alice" than Mr. L—— walked on board. Alice ran to him, and threw her arms around his neck, exclaiming, "My dear father!" She was so much overcome by the unexpected joyous surprise, that she fainted in his arms. But Dr. A——, who was an old acquaintance of Mr. L——, came to the rescue; and Alice was soon restored again.

Mr. L—— then handed Capt. Shields two letters. One was from his dear sister Mary: the other was directed to Miss Annie B. Bird, to the care of Capt. John Shields, commander of the ship "Mary Alice," at London.

We will give our readers a brief synopsis of Annie's letter from the Rev. Mr. B——, whom her mother had

appointed executor of her will. His letter ran thus:
"Miss Bird, your mother, when she made her will, appointed me her executor. Your dear mother died very
suddenly the 1st of last April, and she has left to you
all her property. Her husband died on his passage to
England, where he was then going to receive a large
estate which had fallen to him by the death of a very
rich uncle; and his death had prevented his widow from
receiving any thing from that vast property until only a
month before her death. She called upon me for counsel,
and she did reserve and give several hundred dollars for
benevolent objects, and, had she lived, would have given
more. She died very suddenly; and her last words
were, 'Dear friend, protect and save my dear Annie.'
I now hold in my hand the keys of those treasures, which
are all yours; and I await your orders for their invest-
ment or disposal, till I can turn them over to you their
rightful owner."

This announcement called all the Shieldses and Mr.
L—— together, to advise Annie what reply she should
make to the Rev. Mr. B——'s letter. Mr. Albert Shields
and Mr. L—— were both thorough-going practical busi-
ness-men and good financiers. One proposed, that after
their marriage, which was now soon to be celebrated, they
take the first steamer for B——. To this Annie said she
could never consent: she could not leave her dear cousin
Alice and Johnny; and Mr. L—— said, "I think it would
be well for Annie to telegraph him to keep all the moneys
not invested in the banks until her return." The despatch
was sent, and in a few days a satisfactory answer received.

Two days after, "The Mary Alice" was covered with
bunting from the truck to the deck; and on the afternoon
of Nov. 1 Mr. Ernest Shields was married to Miss Annie
Bliss Bird. After the ceremony had been performed, Alice
threw her arms around Annie's neck, and, giving her
a telling kiss, exclaimed, "My dear blissful bird, I rejoice in believing you will be ever shielded in the future."
Annie expressed her thanks for good wishes; and one
after another came to steal a kiss from her rosy lips.
Finally Mr. Albert Shields came, and threw his strong
arms around the neck of the beautiful bird, exclaiming,

" My dear young sister, the first and all the sister I have, accept a brother's love, a brother's confidence, and his lifelong sympathy for you, which, under God, have been the means of my restoration to the forgiving love of that Saviour from whom I had so far wandered away." Capt. Shields embraced Annie, and said, " My own dear double cousin, I cannot find words to express the joy which this hour affords me ; and my gratitude toward the Bestower of all these joys cannot be told by any human tongue. After partaking of a princely collation, provided by Mr. L——, owner of " The Mary Alice," the wedding-party retired.

In a few more days their cargo was all discharged. Mr. L—— said to Capt. Shields, " Freights from London to B—— are very low indeed ; and it would be of great value, in preserving the frame and timbers of ' The Mary Alice,' to go to St. Ubes, and load her with salt, which is in very fair demand in B——." Capt. Shields said it would be an excellent plan. He then remarked, " She is, I believe, the best ship now afloat upon the ocean. I hope I shall not worship her ; but she seems more to me like a living thing than any ship I ever saw, and she is almost idolized by all my men."

Before sailing, Alice wrote her sister Mary, acquainting her with her new-found cousins, and of Annie's marriage to Mr. Ernest Shields, her own cousin, and giving her a bird's-eye view of their voyage generally. Mr. Albert Shields fulfilled his promise to his brother Ernest, giving him ten thousand dollars to begin with. The final leavetaking between Albert Shields and his wife, and his brother Ernest and his dear Annie, was very touching and tender.

Every thing being ready, " The Mary Alice " sailed from London for St. Ubes in November ; and, after a passage of ten days, they arrived there in safety. Mr. L—— one day, promenading with his daughter, said to her, " Alice, your husband embodies more truly excellent traits of character than I think I ever saw before in any one human composition. Mr. Albert Shields spoke of the quiet and yet decided manner in which he stopped that mutiny without any one's knowing it, — in the night, too,

— and said he was astonished at his far-seeing sagacity, his ever-ready inventive ingenuity, and his decision, and, above all, his daily, living, active, practical piety. I do not blame you for being proud of him."

" Well, my dear father, in order to know how to appreciate Johnny's value, you must live with him. No living woman can be more loving, tender, kind, sympathetic, and forbearing than he is; and, when an emergency occurs, he rises at once, and towers above every difficulty that is connected with it." Her father remarked he did not know but he loved Johnny more than he did her. " That is right, my dear father. Go on. The more you love my Johnny, the more of it I shall get; for you never saw a couple more unselfishly one than Johnny and myself. He but seldom attempts to do any thing without consulting me, unless he has a mutiny to quell in the night." Dr. A—— and his wife soon joined them upon the quarter-deck; and the doctor said to Mr. L——, " I wish to congratulate you, my life-long friend, in your noble ship, ' The Mary Alice,' and in her still more noble commander. I have been with him the whole voyage round, sir, and have seen him under all the varied and sometimes trying circumstances which have environed him, and have never seen him, at any period during this long voyage of more than a year, at loss for a moment what to do, and how to do it. His prudent and thoughtful sagacity in Melbourne, while there, when that terrible epidemic was raging, is one instance. He would not allow any person to leave the ship but himself; neither would he allow any person to come on board from the shore ; and, by so doing, he saved all but himself from that fearful scourge."

" The Mary Alice " sailed from St. Ubes for B—— Dec. 6, 1855 ; and Capt. Shields thought it best to take what is called the middle passage, so as not to have his men exposed to the more severe weather of a more northern passage in mid-winter. After passing the Azores one morning, with a fresh gale blowing from the south-west, the ship being under double-reefed topsails, and a heavy, deep-rolling sea from the westward, — which is most always found in the Atlantic Ocean, — a man aloft sang out, " Sail ho! about two points of the lee-bow, sir." A report was instantly made to Capt. Shields, who ordered the ship kept off two points. Capt. Shields took his glass, and, after looking a moment, said to his officer, "Have the larbord quarter-boat ready for lowering, sir: she may need assistance." — "Her main and mizzen masts are both gone, sir." — "Send Mr. Carter to me at once, sir." Mr. Carter came aft; and Capt. Shields said to Mr. Carter, "I want you to call Joe, Sam, Dick, and Jim, the most experienced men on board; go to that wrecked stranger, and afford all the assistance they may need; keep two men in the boat to take care of her; go on board, and then act according to your own judgment."

"The Mary Alice" was hove to a quarter of a mile from the wrecked ship. The boat was lowered, and they came under her lee. Mr. Carter found she rolled so deep, that he could not board her on the side, without swamping his boat. He ordered his men to pull up under her stern; and the brave Mr. Jack Carter, determining to accomplish his mission, laid hold of a rope hanging over the stern of the wreck, and in a moment was on board. He said, "Now, boys, keep clear of the ship till I see whether there is any living soul here to tell their sad tale of woe." Having given his men their orders, he started to go forward, and saw a man slipping down from the foretop on a spar rope; and, when within ten feet of the deck, he fell. Mr. Carter was at his side in a moment; but the man was so much reduced and exhausted, that he could not speak. Mr. Carter took him in his brawny arms as though he had been an infant, carried him to the stern, and ordered the boat to come as near as it was safe for them. He then took his knife, and cut off as much rope as he needed, and threw one end into the boat; and Joe caught it. He then said, "I will lower this man down, and bend the other end of this rope to him, and you can haul him into the boat. Now, do just as I order, and we will save this poor sufferer." Mr. Carter lowered him down, and Joe in a moment had him in his arms. Mr. Carter said, "Shove off now, boys: don't mind me." Joe said, "You are not going to stop there, sir, are you, Mr. Carter?" — "No. Shove off

that boat." They obeyed orders ; and Mr. Carter leaped
into the sea, swam to the boat, and in a moment was on
board. "Out oars, boys, and pull for the ship."

In a few moments they pulled to the leeward of their
ship, hooked on their boat, which was hoisted up, with all
the men in her. The man was taken out upon deck, and
Dr. A—— again came to the rescue. The man was un-
conscious. Dr. A—— gave him something, and in a few
moments he discovered that life was not extinct. In the
mean time "The Mary Alice" was close-hauled by the
wind, leaving the wreck far astern. Very soon it was
seen that the rescued man was making every effort he
could to speak; and finally Dr. A—— understood him to
say there were two men in the foretop. This intelligence
was reported to Capt. Shields, who at once ordered Mr.
Helm to get ready for tacking ship, remarking, "They
shall be saved if it is possible. — Mr. Helm, are you
ready, sir?"—"All ready, sir." He ordered the man at
the wheel to put his helm hard to port, and exclaimed,
"Hard a lee, sir!" "The Mary Alice," always obedient to her helm, came immediately up. When head to
the wind, the captain exclaimed, "Topsails haul!" In
a moment the main and mizzen topsails were braced en-
tirely opposite to what they were before. The captain
then cried out, "Let go and haul, sir! Brace those
head-yards sharp up, sir, and trim every thing snug by
the wind!"

The wreck was then some three miles away. The captain then ordered the same boat, with the same crew,
ready to try, if it were possible, to save those other two
men. The man had so far recovered, that Alice wanted
him brought into the cabin, where she could take care of
him. He had already told Dr. A—— that the two men
were alive when he left the foretop, but were so weak
they could not help themselves. "The Mary Alice" was
again hove to about a quarter of a mile to windward of
the wreck. The boat was lowered in safety, although the
sea was running very high indeed. Mr. Carter requested
one more man; for it would take two men to take care of
the boat. He then ordered Mr. Mainstay to go with
them.

After coming under the stern of the wreck, Mr. Carter said, "I want Mr. Mainstay and Joe to go on board with me; and you, Dick and Sam, take care of the boat." These three fearless men in a few minutes were on board of the wreck, and went forward together. Mr. Carter said, "Mr. Mainstay, I wish you and Joe to go into that foretop, and bend a rope to them, and lower them down carefully to me, and I will receive them." In a few minutes one was received by Mr. Carter, and was laid in as safe a place as he could find, for the sea was making a complete breach over the wrecked ship. In a few moments more the other man was in Mr. Carter's arms; and the two men hastened down from the top. They carried the two men to the stern, as before; and Joe and Mr. Mainstay got into the boat to receive the men. Mr. Carter lowered first one, and then the other, into the boat, and got in himself. They then pulled for the ship, and were all very soon on board "The Mary Alice," and she again was put on her way towards her destined haven. Dr. A—— took charge of the two men, and gave them something that soon produced signs of life; and Alice soon made room for them in the cabin. She said, "These poor fellows have suffered enough: I will give them my own bed, and I can lie on one of the sofas. They shall have my time, my care, and my prayers; for I expect they have a narrative to disclose when they get able to do it, if they live. I believe our dear old tars who have perilled their lives to save these men will to-night add their faith in prayer to their self-sacrificing labors; and the two united God will not turn away."

Mr. L—— was perfectly delighted in seeing the practical piety of his two only dear children. He said he had not taken so much comfort, and so enjoyed himself spiritually, as he had done since they left London, for many years; and he added, "My dear Johnny, I think I shall go with you on your next voyage." — "Nothing would please me better, my dear father." — "After we arrive in B——, I intend to give you a full bill of sale of 'The Mary Alice,' as your wedding-present." — "I thank you, my ever dear father, and hope the confidence you repose in me may never be regretted. Ever since Jesus pardoned my sins on that never-to-be-forgotten night, it has been my daily desire to do something for Him who has done so much for me; and during this long voyage I have tried, as far as possible, to carry out the principle of love to God and man to all within the circle of my ship's family."

Mary Alice, jun., occupied many of the leisure hours of her loving grandfather L——. One day they saw a schooner, with her ensign hoisted union down; and Capt. Shields said she wanted help of some kind he had no doubt. "The Mary Alice" soon came up with her, and hailed, "What schooner is that? and do you want aid?" The reply was, "It is the schooner 'Rapid,' from Barbadoes, bound to B—— ; and we are in want of water." Capt. Shields ordered a cask filled, slung, and thrown overboard. A. boat was then lowered, and the cask towed to the schooner, for which they seemed very grateful; and the boat returned, and was hoisted up, and all sail was made upon "The Mary Alice," pressing her through the briny deep with grandeur and rapidity.

Their evening meetings were very interesting; and Mr. L—— enjoyed them as much as any person on board. He said to Dr. A——, "I shall never forget the prayer-meeting they had the evening after meeting that wrecked ship. When I heard those hardy sons of the ocean plead as they did with God to restore to life and health those they had that day saved from starvation and death, and saw those great briny tears trickling down their weather-beaten faces, I felt like hiding my face in shame at my own want of that deep sympathy which I saw manifested by Capt. Shields and his men, whom he so much loves. I never knew before that sailors had such deep and ardent feelings for suffering humanity." Dr. A—— replied, saying, "I have learned more of the loveliness and self-sacrificing traits of their character than I ever knew before. They have a frank open-heartedness, associated with a woman's tenderness. They are bold, daring, and brave; and yet their tears will flow in a moment at seeing human sufferings. I know of no class of people who possess so many excellent traits of charac-

ter as our seamen; and yet how much they are abused,
neglected, and despised by many of our people!"—
"Alas! it is too true, Dr. A——. But I confess to
you frankly, my dear sir, that I was not aware, till on
this passage, that they possessed so many very excellent
traits of character."—"Neither was I; but this long
and very pleasant voyage has banished all doubts in that
direction, and fully converted me to the espousal of the
sailor's cause all the rest of my life."—"Well, how are
those three men getting along?" Dr. A—— said, "They
are getting along nicely, and will soon be well; and I
think they will have a sad tale of woe to tell as soon as
they are able."

The sabbath that next dawned upon them was indeed
a lovely day. At ten A.M. the bell had.no sooner struck
four than all hands gathered aft. After singing, prayer,
and reading the Scriptures by Capt. Shields, he then remarked that the three rescued men would meet with
them, and, by the permission of Dr. A——, would tell
the whole narrative of their voyage.

One of them arose, and said, "The ship 'Rambler'
sailed from St. John, N.B., Dec. 6, commanded by Capt.
H——. We had two mates, cook, steward, and ten
men. She was laden with timber and plank, bound for
Liverpool. After passing Cape Sable in the Gulf, we
experienced some heavy north-east gales, which caused
unusual heavy labor for our ship; and we found she had
sprung a leak. We afterwards had strong westerly gales
and a heavy sea; and we found that the water in the
ship's hold was gaining upon us, with both pumps going
night and day. Capt. H—— ordered the mainmast to
be cut away, hoping to relieve the ship in some measure.
The mainmast fell with an awful crash upon the mizzenmast, and broke it off about fifteen feet from the deck;
and we cut away the rigging and spars, that we might
clear them from the ship. We kept the ship before the
wind under a close-reefed foretopsail and reefed foresail; and, water-logged as we were, we could only make
about three miles per hour. Being lumber-laden, we
knew she could not sink; and we hoped we might possibly
get across the Atlantic, if she did not come to pieces.

As near as I can remember, about ten days after, the wind changed to the north-east, and blew a furious gale. Before we could furl our foresail and foretopsail, the wind, which became very violent, blew every thread of canvas from the yards, and the ship lay in the trough of the sea, which very soon washed overboard all our officers and most of our men; while the huge weight of water in the ship's hold was bursting off one deck-plank after another until the whole deck was torn up, and only we three were left. We repaired to the foretop to get out of the way of the sea, that had swallowed in its open throat all our shipmates; and I had just strength enough that morning to stand up, and take what I expected my last look, when I spied you steering very near for us. I told my shipmates. Only one spoke; and his words were, ' It is too late.' But when you hove to the windward of us, and lowered your boat, I was so afraid that you would not come up into the foretop, that I was determined you should see us, and I laid hold of a rope, making it fast round the masthead, and started to slip down that rope, to tell the brave fellows that there were two more in the top. My strength and all failed me, and I fell, and knew nothing more till I found myself here; and, when I did know any thing, L told this dear good doctor there were two more in the top. I think, if I remember aright, that we divided and ate our last biscuit five days ago. I believe I have told you all, and you know the rest. And now I want you to pray for me, that God may have mercy on my soul; for I told him in that water-logged ship's foretop, if he would save my life, that I would give him the rest of my days, either few or many. I have heard you pray every night; and I have just longed to tell you all, I have been a great sinner. I know Jesus Christ came into the world to save sinners; but I fear I have passed the rubicon of his mercy."

Mr. Mainstay said, " Capt. Shields, I just want to say a word or two to my dear shipmate. — I believe you said you feared you had passed something. I suppose you meant you was afraid you was too late, like your shipmates in the top." — "That's it, shipmate: you have it." — "Well, now, if you have any fears, it is pretty sure the Lord has not given you up, shipmate; for, if he had given you up, you would not have any fears about the matter. If you want to discharge that cargo of sin that you have been a lifetime loading up, you had better not try to hoist out a barrel at a time, but just go to Jesus, and tell him how sorry you are (if you be sorry), and ask him to unload your soul, and then believe he will do it. I tell you, shipmate, he will discharge your whole cargo in less than a minute. That is the way he unloaded this old hull, and a wickeder man never lived than I have been."

After Mr. Mainstay had done speaking, Capt. Shields said, "If there is any other man here that wishes to be remembered in our prayers, if he will speak out we will carry him in our arms of faith to Jesus." The other two men who had been rescued said no men needed prayers more than they did, and none deserved them less; for they had been great sinners all their lives. They never had got on board of a praying ship before. They said they did not know much about heaven, but thought this ship must be something like it, for they had heard no swearing by either officers or men.

Capt. Shields then said, "Let us all kneel before the Lord our Maker." He offered a fervent prayer, and was followed by the first and second officers, and Joe and Sam and Dick, Mr. Carter having charge of the deck. When Mr. Mainstay prayed, all were bathed in tears. His homely yet fervent pleading inportunity laid fast hold of the promise, saying, —

> "Lord, we cannot let thee go
> Till salvation thou bestow:
> Lord, let it come like a shower
> On my shipmates this very hour;
> And we will praise thee every day,
> While we in this world shall stay."

"And, blessed Jesus, thou shalt have all the glory, forever. Amen." They then sang Mr. Mainstay's favorite hymn, found in another part of this narrative; and Capt. Shields dismissed the meeting, saying he expected gracious results from this praying-hour.

Mr. L——, after they had retired, said, "My dear son, never have I experienced such a profitable hour." Alice

said, " We have had many such."   Annie said, " I have
learned more how to trust from these praying sailors than
I ever knew before ; but did you ever see any thing equal
to Mr. Mainstay's prayer and his poetry?"   Alice said,
" I hope he will never leave this ship."   Capt. Shields
said he did not mean he ever should, nor Joe nor Sam
nor Dick, nor Mr. Carter.

CHAPTER VIII.

LITTLE Mary Alice was now over eight months old, and could stand up by taking hold of things, and was the pet of all hands on board. Three days after, the man aloft sung out, "Land ho! right ahead, sir!"

With the wind fair and a good breeze, "The Mary Alice" in a few hours passed by the Highland Lighthouse, and shaped her course west-north-west for B—— Lighthouse. Three hours after, they took a pilot, and at four P.M. came to anchor in the stream, just abreast of Granite Wharf, arriving Jan. 7, 1856, after a passage of twenty-eight days from St. Ubes, having been gone one year and two months, and having circumnavigated the ·globe since they left B——.

All the crew and passengers remained on board; it being so late, none wished to leave the ship. Dr. A—— said the next morning, he regretted that all the pleasures of that never-to-be-forgotten voyage were now terminated. That night, laying within three hundred yards of the wharf, not one soul wished to leave the ship; and that evening there were more tears shed than ever before. Each one felt that on the morrow there would be a separation which would be painful to bear. The captain, his officers, and men, had lived together like a great Christian family, as they were. About eight bells all hands retired for rest. In the morning Capt. Shields and Mr. L—— went on shore together. After transacting his business at the custom-house, he found the ship "Swiftsure" had arrived, and Capt. B—— had declined going again. Mr. L—— offered the command of "The Swiftsure" to Mr. Helm; which he gladly accepted, and proposed, if there was no objection, to taking Mr. Carter for his first officer; which was agreed to by all parties. Two days afterwards the ship "Swiftsure" sailed for Bremen.

The second day after the arrival of " The Mary Alice,"
she was hauled in to the wharf; and yet Capt. Shields had
said nothing about discharging any of his men.   He said
to Mr. Boom, " I wish you, sir, to fill the office of first
officer in the place of Mr. Helm, now master of the ship
' Swiftsure.'—Mr. Mainstay, you will fill the office va-
cated by Mr. Boom."   He then called Joe aft, and said,
" Well, Joe, my good fellow, I want you to fill my third
officer's place, made vacant by the promotion of Mr.
Carter."   He called for Sam, and said, " I wish you to
accept the office of boatswain;" which he gladly accepted.   He then called his men aft, and said he would
not discharge a single man that wished to remain by the
ship.   Only two men wished to be discharged; and their
places were readily filled by the three men they had taken
from the wrecked ship.   He then told Mr. Boom he
wanted all the sails unbent, and such as needed repairing
to be taken between decks, and set the best of the men
at work under Mr. Mainstay.   Mr. Windlass (who had
been Joe) and Sam (now Mr. Forestay) were to see to
refitting the ship's rigging, with such men as they needed.
The balance were employed in trimming the salt into the
hatchways, ready for discharging by the stevedore.   Capt.
Shields gave orders to Mr. Boom in regard to ballast
when it was needed, and, after giving all necessary orders
said, " I shall be absent perhaps for ten days, and leave
you in sole charge, sir.   Take good care of ' The Mary
Alice ' till my return."   He then bade all his men good-
by, and went home to his father's.

Mr. L—— said, " I had wanted to invite all those
noble men to my house, and give them as sumptuous a
feast as I could." — " Better time to do that, my dear
father, when we return." Alice wanted a maid.   Capt.
Shields said, " You had better get a good country-girl."
— " I guess you are right, my dear Johnny."

The next morning Johnny and Alice and her babe, and
Mr. Ernest Shields and his dear Annie, and Mr. L——,
took the train for B——, where they arrived at noon.
After partaking of an excellent dinner, Mr. L—— said
he wished the landlord to provide a large, comfortable
carriage, with four good horses, to carry their whole party

to G——; and then said he should want them to bring them to B——, and he would write when to send for them. They were soon under way towards G——, arriving there at four P.M., and there was a very warm greeting between them all. Then Alice said, "I now have the unspeakable pleasure of introducing to Mr. Merritt and his wife their own dear and double cousins, Mr. Ernest Shields and his wife, my ever blissful Annie."

After a very warm greeting, Mrs. Merritt, familiarly known as Mary, Capt. Shields's only sister, said, "I think this introduction to these new double cousins, as sister Alice calls them, needs some little explanation; for I am sure my husband and myself are in the dark about this matter." — "Now, sister Mary, I want you to stop and think before you answer the question I am about to ask." — "Ask on, dear Alice: I am all attention." — "Do you, or do you not, remember of hearing your dear mother say any thing to you about your aunt Annie?" Mary instantly said yes, — said she was five years older than she, was living somewhere in the northern part of the State; "but, if she ever told me the name of the town, I have forgotten it." — "Now, this is her only child and daughter. Her husband is your own father's brother's son; and their being married as they were in London makes them your double cousins." — "Yes; but, Alice dear, how does my cousin Annie get to London?" — "Why, she has been the whole voyage round with us." — "Well, that I can understand." And the very inquisitive Mary must be told the whole story before she could be satisfied.

Mr. Merritt said, "Ladies and gentlemen, you must excuse me. It is the evening for our regular prayer-meeting, and I am expecting to hear the bell every moment." Alice said, "My dear brother, I shall not excuse you, for I am going to that meeting myself, if I can find any among these good sister-helpers of yours, my dear sister, that will take care of Mary Alice." One young lady said she would stop, and take care of her child; but, if she should awake, she might be afraid of a stranger. Alice said, "She is a regular bred sailor, and fears no one: if she can only find some one to play with her, she will be satisfied." — "Then," said the young lady, "I will cheerfully volunteer my services."

The tolling bell soon called them all to the house of prayer. After Mr. Merritt had offered a brief prayer, they began singing "Rock of Ages;" and when Alice and Annie and Mr. Ernest Shields blended their voices with them, they made the place ring as it had not for some time before. After singing, Mr. Merritt read the account of Jesus healing the sick of palsy. Capt. Shields said, since he met with them some eighteen months since, he had seen many sin-palsied souls forever cured of the palsy of sin in its worst forms. Mr. L—— then arose, and said he could bear testimony to the truth of Capt. Shields's remarks; for he had been an eye-witness to such displays of Jesus' love as he had never seen before. Then Mr. Ernest Shields said he had never seen such wonderful displays of Jesus' power to save sinners as he had seen on board the ship "Mary Alice." Annie then said, "'The Mary Alice' I shall never forget: it was from those rough tars, whom I shall ever love, that I learned my first lesson of simple childlike love and trust in Jesus." Alice then rose and said, "Dear brethren and sisters, I little thought, when we were last here, that in my whole life I should ever be permitted to see what I have seen, and hear what I have heard, and feel and enjoy what I have felt and enjoyed; and, if it were not for prolonging your meeting beyond its ordinary limits, I should like to tell you of some of the wonders of God's power upon the ocean." She was about to sit down, when a dozen voices all at once exclaimed, "Go on, dear sister: we will stay till morning to hear you." She then said, "I will briefly tell you of one case." And she went on to describe the ignorance of the man, and then his wickedness, according to his own statement; how she and her sister Shields had agreed to pray all night for him if he would pray, and of his sending them word at midnight that the work was done. And then Annie and Alice struck up and sung the song he had composed and sung that night he was converted. When she had finished, many of them were bathed in tears: they wished to obtain a copy of that sweet song. They then all rose, and sung the Doxology, and were dismissed.

After they had got home, Mary said, "Dear Alice, why did you stop? You acted all the time as though you must hurry, and abbreviate your narrative. Now, those men and women meant what they said, when they said they would stay till morning; and I am sure I could. Oh! it was so interesting, and so well calculated to encourage and strengthen the faith of all of God's people! But I will try to be grateful for what I did get, and shall expect more from you next time."—"Well, my own sweet sister Mary," said Alice, "the next opportunity I have, I will try to make you twice glad." After having their evening devotions, they all retired for the night. The next morning after breakfast, they first visited the cemetery, and stood beside the graves of their parents. Capt. Shields, leaning over the stone at his mother's grave, said,-"I must give utterance to my overloaded heart." And he spake amid his tears, "'My prayers will be answered: God will save you, my dear boy.' These were the dying-words of my now sainted mother. They have been answered in my own salvation. But look, and measure the effects of those prayers upon other hearts, and their influence again over the minds of others; and that influence will never cease until the last sinner is saved." He then knelt between the two graves, and poured out his full soul for God to guide, to teach, to lead, and control him in all his future history.

They then visited together their old home where they were born, the room where his mother died, the blacksmith's shop where his dear father once toiled to earn bread for his family. As he, with his wife on his arm, looked at all these things, he said, "Every thing of my past history is a living present to-day. All my boyish freaks with my precious sister — even the sounding of the horn from that attic-window you see yonder, the fatal pitchfork, and my cowardly running away and leaving that loving sister alone and unprotected, if I could, in my selfishness save myself — meet me here to-day."— "Why, Johnny, I think you never told me the reasons why you left the country for a sea-life." — "Neither did I think it necessary, my dear Alice, to tell you all the evil things which I have done: it would be a much larger volume of my history than I should care to have you read just now, Alice dear."

The next day was the holy sabbath, which was both clear and cold; and Mr. Merritt said, after their morning devotions, "I have always made it my practice to endeavor to present truth in the quality and quantity which I thought best calculated to promote my people's spirituality. You all saw the deep interest with which they listened to our dear sister Alice and cousin Annie at our last prayer-meeting. I propose, therefore, with your consent, that you agree among yourselves the part each shall take in telling us, in your own way, the most interesting portion of your late voyage. I shall preach this morning, and, with your consent, will tell my people of the afternoon programme."

They all agreed to brother Merritt's proposal; and Alice then said, "I would give a hundred dollars if Mr. Mainstay was here this morning." Her father said, "I would give five hundred; for I believe he would do more good than all of us put together." — "The bell is ringing, and we must soon be on our way to meeting," said Mr. Merritt, "for I like to be prompt as to time." Mr. L—— said that little could be accomplished in this world without system; and they left the parsonage for the house of worship. As this group of visitors entered the church, led by their pastor, the whole congregation arose, and remained standing till all had been seated. The choir then sung a hymn of welcome, and all was silent. Mr. Merritt offered an invocation, returning thanks for past blessings, and earnestly imploring present aid. After singing, Mr. Merritt read the fifth chapter of second Corinthians, and then poured out his full soul in such a trusting and yet importuning prayer, that all were melted and subdued. After singing again, he announced the first verse of the chapter he had read as his text: "For we know, if this earthly house of our tabernacle were dissolved, we have a building of God, an house not made with hands, eternal in the heavens." He first described the beauty, strength, and utility of our bodies; but, as they were material, they would be dissolved by *death;* secondly, he showed the vast importance of securing the knowledge in the text.

He then said God had made the provision so ample, that none need to die without an assurance of that knowledge, and urged all to seek it then and there. Delays were dangerous, time short, and life uncertain ; and what was done to secure a preparation must be done quickly.

Mr. Merritt then said, "We have several old, tried friends with us to-day, who this afternoon will give us some reminiscences of their late voyage around the globe." In the afternoon the house was well filled ; and Alice handed Mr. Merritt quite a package, saying, "Please hand it to the chorister." She had, on the voyage, adapted the music to the words of Bill's hymn ; and she and Annie had sung it at the prayer-meeting, and she had prepared these copies agreeably to their request. The meeting opened with a voluntary on the part of the choir ; and a fervent prayer was then offered by Mr. L——. Mr. Merritt then read the hundred and seventh psalm, or that portion relating to seamen, found from the twenty-third to thirty-second verses.

Capt. Shields then arose, and in a brief manner related the most interesting events which occurred from B—— to San Francisco. Then Annie arose, and related with great precision the events from San Francisco to Melbourne, involving Alice's confinement, and the mutiny and how it was quelled, and the number of souls converted ; and, before she completed her recital, all wept like children. After singing a hymn, Alice arose, and said, "From Melbourne to London, nothing unusual occurred, except the conversion of several of our men. In London our dear cousin who last spoke to you was married ; and in a few days we sailed for St. Ubes, and from that place to B——. On our passage to B——, one day we espied a vessel ; and, as we drew nearer, we saw she was a wreck. Two of her masts were gone ; and we sent our boat to her, although there was a heavy sea running. And three men, by our dear, daring, and self-sacrificing men, were taken from the foretop of that floating wreck, brought on board of our ship, restored to consciousness and health ; and, better than all, before we reached B—— all three of those men were regenerated by the Spirit's power, and made to rejoice in a Savior's forgiving love."

After Alice had sat down, an aged man arose, and said, "Dear brethren, how this daring bravery of risking their own lives to seek and save others is like the love of Jesus dying for us! and how it puts to blush our indifference in behalf of our wives, children, and friends! I feel to-day, from what I have heard, like hiding my face in the dust before God, to implore him to forgive my sins, and constrain me to do my duty better in the future." Several others spoke; and then Bill's favorite hymn was sung, which, with the aid of the organ, moved every heart. That evening they had a very interesting meeting.

The next morning, having exchanged several letters with the Rev. Mr. B—— of D——, Mr. Shields said it was really necessary for him and his wife to leave them, to attend to his wife's business. The leave-taking was tender and tearful. It was very hard for Alice to part with Annie. She seemed to her as an own sister. They had loved each other with all the warmth of sisterly affection.

After Annie and her husband had left, Capt. Shields said they would have to return to B—— on the morrow; that his business was such, that it could not be longer neglected. Alice had employed as her maid Miss Susan Hall, the young lady that took care of her child the evening she attended the prayer-meeting. Alice's sister Mary had a little daughter, which she had named Alice Bliss Merritt; and there was only one week's difference in the ages of Alice's and Mary's children. The next morning, after breakfast, at their morning devotions fervent prayers were laid upon God's altar for his blessing upon each one present, and for Annie and her husband; and the leave-taking was not only solemn, but it was touching and tender. Capt. Shields, embracing his dear sister, said, "Dear Mary, there will be a last time that we shall meet. As we do not know when it will come, and as this may be the last time we may ever see each other, I now present to you, my only dear sister, this memento of your only brother John and sister Alice." The memento was a large, beautiful gold locket, with a perfect likeness of himself and wife. He then gave her another, with the picture of his father Mr. L——, and their darling Mary

Alice. Mary said she had no words to express her gratitude for the two lockets, and hoped she should be able some day to repay them for these tokens of esteem and affection. The carriage had arrived; and Capt. Shields and wife, and Mr. L——, and Susan with Mary Alice, entered the carriage. The final good-by was spoken; and they started on their way to B——, where they took the train for their city home, where they arrived about noon. Capt. Shields immediately repaired to his ship; and Mr. Boom gave him a warm reception, as did all his men. Mr. Boom reported all he had done, — the cargo had been discharged, every sail put in first-rate repair, besides making one new topsail, and the ship's rigging was ready for another year's wear. Capt. Shields expressed his entire satisfaction with all that had been done during his absence. A few days after, Capt. Shields had a freight offered him to the Isle of France, or Mauritius, and from there to Manilla, and back to B——. In a few days he had accepted their proposals, and filled the ship's lower hold with all kinds of lumber and timber for building-purposes; and between decks was filled with all kinds of ship's spars of different sizes. In a few more days "The Mary Alice" was ready for sea. Three new men were shipped to fill up the complement. Capt. Shields and his wife, with Susan and Mary Alice, jun., with Mr. L——, came on board; and Dr. A—— said it would cost no more for him to board on the ship than in the city. Capt. Shields said, "Dr. A——, if you will go with me on this voyage, it shall not cost you a cent. My father, I know, will assent to this proposal." Mr. L—— said, "I shall certainly consent to any thing the captain proposes to do."

Dr. A—— and his wife, with their baggage, were soon on board; and the noble "Mary Alice" glided out of the harbor, bound for Mauritius. We now leave her, with our best wishes for her safe return to B—— after she has visited her ports of destination. She sailed March 1, 1856.

It is the author's earnest wish, that all who read this narrative may be impressed with the power and influence which the principles illustrated in this narrative are so well calculated to produce. In the captain of "The Mary Alice" we see a bold, daring bravery; a man of wisdom and decision, equal to the emergency; and all tempered and controlled by a never-flagging love to God and men, that is rarely found, and seldom equalled, and yet is attainable by all. And my only desire is, that every reader of this brief narrative may, through its influence, kindle its soul-saving fire of divine love upon their hearts in such a degree as shall make them all as fruitful as the subjects of this brief work. Consistent, active, daily, practical, self-denying Christians, like the captain of "The Mary Alice," make the world better because they have lived in it.

I now record, in conclusion, the hymn composed and sung at their wedding in B——, in June, 1854, which I noted at the time of their marriage: —

> At the bridal altar now
> We together pledge our vow;
> Record our united love
> In thy register above.
>
> Here we pledge our hearts and hands,
> To be joined in life-long bands;
> And we here accept to-day
> Bonds that bind eternally.
>
> I sought her; she is my bride;
> In her love I now confide:
> Now she is forever mine,
> I to her my heart resign.
>
> His proposal I receive:
> I am his, I now believe.
> He is mine, I ask no more, —
> Mine now and forevermore.
>
> May their lives unspotted be,
> Jesus having set them free!
> Their example ever shine,
> Show religion is divine.
>
> Lord, now ratify their vow
> Which they make before thee now:
> Save from sin and every snare,
> Let them both thy glory share!

T. ATWOOD.

www.ingramcontent.com/pod-product-compliance
Lightning Source LLC
Chambersburg PA
CBHW020039030726
47499CB00007B/2505